Twelve

Twelve

A Retelling of the Twelve Dancing Princesses

Joan Marie Verba

FTL Publications
Minneapolis, Minnesota

FTL Publications
P O Box 22693
Minneapolis, MN 55422-0693
www.ftlpublications.com
mail@ftlpublications.com

Cover art by GetCovers

Printed in the United States of America

ISBN 978-1-936881-71-0

In memory of

Ann Peters

Chapter 1

Alden lifted his head from his pillow and looked north toward the mountains. They seemed no nearer. How long had it been? On the twenty-fifth day after he had left the ancient, abandoned trade route, the wind had snatched away the calendar a monk in Constantinople had given him. He had not been in the mood to track the days since.

He pushed the blanket aside and sat up on his bedroll, scratching his head and rubbing his chin. His rucksack carried a razor, comb, and mirror, but he had not been in the mood to use those lately, either. The stubble had not yet grown into a beard, but would, with time, if he did not shave, soon.

His empty stomach rumbled. While he still had dry bread from the day before, he preferred to see if there was anything nearby he could gather. Although he had a fishing line and hooks, he had yet to see a stream or a pond on this flat land leading to the mountains. Occasional springs or wells along the way kept him supplied with water, as did the ample debris on either side of the road.

These spoils reminded him of what was left in the wake of a rapidly retreating army. Certainly he had, in his past, been part of a force that had been routed, as well as in groups that had gathered the abandoned goods of an army in retreat. He stood to better survey the bounty surrounding him: wooden wheels (broken and whole), blankets, clothing (fine silks to rough wool), and...ah!...crockery. Plates. Utensils. That meant food.

He walked in that direction and rummaged through a pile. Yes...cheese, honey, figs...butter! He sniffed at the contents of a pottery container, dipped a finger in it, and tasted. The butter seemed unspoiled. In fact, he had not yet found rotten food

in his searches. Curious, since he had not seen anyone else
around. Surely if the food was fresh, those abandoning it had
to be close by? He shrugged, gathered his goods, and returned
to his bedroll, where he ate a hearty breakfast. The remnants
he wrapped in a cloth and put in his rucksack. After folding
his blanket and bedroll, and stuffing in his pillow (a welcome
find early in his journey), he shouldered the sack, stepped on
the road, and continued his journey.

About mid-morning, a wagon, a large open wooden box on
wheels drawn by a couple of oxen, came into view, approaching
him from the north. As it approached, Alden could see the driver,
a strongly-built, balding man. Two childish faces peered over
the side of the box. A worn-looking woman rested her back on
the opposite side.

The man drew the oxen to a halt when Alden was opposite
him. The children scrambled out and went exploring.

"No use going on," the man said, without preamble. "There's
nothing there."

Alden looked from the man to the mountains and back again.

"I know," the man said. "You heard the stories about a hidden
kingdom where peace reigned over all. So did I. But we've been
traveling for weeks and still haven't found the place." He inclined
his head northward. "Ever notice the mountains don't seem to
get any closer?"

Alden nodded. "Yes."

"A mirage. It has to be. Finally the wife and I got fed up and
turned back. We'll take up with her family in the Alps. It's not
an easy life, but we'll be spared armies marching through every
few years."

A sudden, loud sound made Alden cringe and cover his ears.

The man turned. "Just one of the young ones dropping a
hammer on the road." He threw Alden a sympathetic look. "Why
not come with us? We have room."

Alden slowly put his hands down, straightened up, and
shook his head.

The man also shook his head. "You won't find anything back
there, believe me. Just more road and more wreckage. Guess a
lot of folks wanting peace and quiet just gave up and ran home
as fast as they could, from the look of things."

"No, travelers would keep whatever supplies they could carry. What I see are signs of an army in headlong retreat, running for their lives."

The man sat back a little. "Yes, I heard that there was some sort of power in the land that struck fear in the hearts of invaders and kept it at peace." He shrugged. "But I tell you, we saw nothing to make us afraid, just more of this." He raised an arm to gesture at their surroundings.

"Godspeed, then, to you and your family."

The man gripped the reins again. "Luck go with you, friend."

Alden nodded and continued walking. Behind him, he heard the man shouting instructions to the children to put what they had gathered into the wagon so they could travel on.

The sun was kind and the weather held. Now that he thought of it, all the time he had been walking, there had been neither fierce heat nor bitter cold. No rain had dampened his cloak. Sometimes a wind would come up, strong enough to snatch anything he held loosely, but with grassland on either side of the road, at least he had not been pelted by sand or grit...and the wind would die down quickly.

He felt he had no choice but to plod on. After years of soldiering, the cannon fire, the report of guns, the screams... had all become unbearable. Once he obtained his last release, he had settled in a town, doing the work of a laborer, but found that any sudden loud noise unnerved him. Nightmares interrupted his sleep. Sometimes at meals he would sit at a table, mindlessly staring at a wall, unaware of any activity around him until a server or barkeep told him to leave.

One day he realized he could not go on this way. He remembered the stories traded around the campfires after a battle. A story that came up more than once was a tale of a kingdom of peace. Once, a comrade even drew out a map. While others scoffed and turned their attention to wineskins, Alden had leaned over while his comrade traced the route on a map— a long-disused route from Constantinople to the empires in the East. As a hired guard, Alden had traveled a similar route from Rome through India with merchants who bought and traded goods. His fellow soldier said he would go there once he had his release and invited Alden to go with him. Alden declined, but when he buried his friend after the next battle, he saved the map. (As soldiers do, they had made a pact that if something happened to one of them, the other could take what they wished.)

Without breaking stride, Alden turned to the mountains again. He felt he had no choice but to reach this legendary realm. His life was no good elsewhere. Even if the land was a fable, even if the supplies at the side of the road ran out, he would keep walking until the end of his life, one way or the other.

One day, in the afternoon, a fog rolled in. He stopped and looked around. He could not see much farther than an arm's reach. The road at his feet was clear, however. He walked ahead slowly, carefully, and soon heard what seemed to be the squeaking of wheels. He had not seen anyone ahead of him earlier, but perhaps he had caught up with someone?

BOOM!

Alden gasped, jumped, and covered his ears. When he put his hands down, he heard a male voice grumbling. Lifting his head, he saw that the fog had dispersed a little. In front of him was a small cart, leaning over to one side. The wheel had come off. A man stood over the wheel, looking down, arm gripping the side of the cart.

Alden walked over. Examining the axle, he said, "The wheel isn't broken. We should be able to put it back on. The pin just broke."

The man sighed and faced Alden. "If we can find a pin. And the tools. And lift up the cart to put it back on. I'm afraid I don't have the strength I did in my younger days."

"Let me see what I can do." He looked into the cart. "Do you have anything? A staff?"

The man shook his head. "Just finished my deliveries for the day and am on my way home."

"Let me see if there's something at the side of the road."

"Hah. As if there are treasures there."

"You never know." The fog seemed to have lifted a little more and light seemed to be shining through. He took off his rucksack and set it at the side of the road before looking around. The man was right; there did not seem as much debris as before. Still, on just about any road he had ever traveled, there would be something. Scrounging, he picked up broken boards which might be pulled apart for shoring up the axle or using as pins. When his hands were full, he put the boards in the cart, and saw a long peg there, and a hammer. Thinking that the man had simply forgotten they were there, he took them, and the boards. Using some nearby rocks, and Alden's strong shoulder, the two of them managed to lift the axle, put on the wheel, and insert the peg.

When they were finished, the man dusted off his hands. "Thanks, stranger. Lucky you found that peg and the hammer."

"Aren't they yours? I got them from the cart."

He shook his head. "No, my cart was empty."

"Maybe you forgot?"

"Haven't seen that hammer before."

Alden thought maybe a family member or customer had put it in without the man knowing. In any case, it was not a matter worth arguing over. "I'll just leave it with you." He put it in the cart. "You might need it again."

"Thank you, friend." He appraised Alden curiously. "You new here?"

Alden nodded.

"We do get folks coming in from time to time. Here, come sit up in front with me and I'll drop you at a place where you can get room and board."

The sun came out. Alden looked up...and up...and up.

The man followed his gaze. "Not seen mountains before, friend?"

That morning, the mountains had seemed far away as ever. Now, they appeared to be only a few miles away.

The man waited patiently as Alden collected himself.

"Oh, yes," Alden said at last. "Much obliged. Thank you."

The man drove to a sturdy-looking inn and drew to a halt. Alden took his rucksack and jumped off. They exchanged a friendly wave and warm farewells. Alden stepped off the road and the man traveled on.

As Alden shouldered his rucksack, he looked around. The stone streets, he saw as they had traveled, were remarkably clean. The raised walkways at the edge of the streets were also clean. They were not crowded, but not empty, either. People walked to their destinations, singly or in groups, going in and out of shop doors or pausing to look at wares through windows. Clothing varied, but most wore what Alden was familiar with through his travels: breeches and boots, shirts and coats, skirts and dresses. None paused to stare at him, which was a relief.

He pushed the door of the inn until it opened and stepped inside. Several wooden tables stood empty, with chairs pushed in around them. At his right stood a counter where five men sat. Behind the counter, a man turned to him and gestured with an arm.

"There he is, men, the next king of the realm!"

Alden turned. Had someone come in behind him? No, the door had closed and latched. He turned back to the speaker.

"Yes, you! I mean you! King of the realm!"

The men at the counter raised mugs and grinned. "To the next king of the realm!"

Chapter 2

Alden glanced behind him once more to be sure no one had followed him inside. He faced the man behind the counter again. "I don't know who you mean, but it can't be me."

"Aren't you new here?"

"I am."

"Didn't you come here to take the hand of a princess?"

Alden shook his head. "Not me. I came here only for a meal and a bed."

The counterman inclined his head. "Those we have." He gestured to the empty tables. "Take a chair. There'll be dinner after Jacob arrives. Do you have coin?"

Alden removed his rucksack and set it on a chair. The chair next to it faced the counter; he sat. Reaching inside his jacket, he took out his purse. Loosening the drawstrings, he poured some coins in his hand. "What sort of coins do you take?" He stood, walked to the counter, and set the coins there.

The counterman scrutinized them and nodded. "Aye, we take these." He reached under the counter and brought out a scale. "We go by weight here." He put small counterweights of varying sizes on one plate and one of Alden's gold coins on the other, taking counterweights on and off until they balanced.

He looked up at Alden. "That will pay for food and bed for a month."

Alden took the remaining coins and put them back in his purse and tucked the purse back into his jacket.

The counterman put the coin, weights, and scale under the counter again. He held out a hand. "My name's Quentin, by the way."

Alden clasped his hand briefly. "Alden."

Quentin also released his grip and gestured to the man on the other side of the counter nearest Alden. "That's Bennu."

Bennu had short, straight gray hair. He, too, clasped hands with Alden.

Quentin gestured to the man next to him. He had a wrinkled face and short black curly hair streaked with gray. "This is Khalil." Alden took a step around Bennu and clasped hands with him.

Quentin continued with the introductions. "Gerasim." Another gray-haired man.

"Deval."

"Timicin."

When he had greeted all the others, Alden returned to his seat. He had noted that all the men were significantly older than he; even Quentin had some gray in his brown hair.

When Alden was seated, Bennu turned to him. "So you didn't come here to marry a princess?"

He shook his head. "Never entered my mind. I'm a landless younger son of an estate holder."

Bennu looked at him sympathetically. "You'll fit right in here."

Gerasim took a swig of the tankard in front of him and turned to Alden. "Truly. You hadn't heard of the king's offer?"

"First I've heard of it was from you."

Quentin said, "Well, then, you may as well know, since you're here. The king here, King Reginald, has twelve daughters."

"Twelve," Bennu emphasized. "No sons."

"The girls started getting to the age where the young bucks were noticing them," Quentin continued. "To put a stop to it, he moved them all from the family quarters to the side of the castle that abuts the mountains."

"It's very nice there," Bennu said. "I was hired to plant the trees and flowers in the garden myself, years ago. The rooms overlook the garden, the mountain, and the whole southern half of the kingdom. There's quite a view."

"Yes, a very nice prison," Quentin said. "There's only one way in and out of that section of the castle. The king himself locks the doors to the hall every evening and unlocks it every morning."

Gerasim held up a finger. "Except. Every morning when the door is opened, all of their shoes are lined up by the door. Every shoe is worn out."

"The princesses have nothing to say about it," Khalil said. "King Reginald has begged, pleaded, threatened, lost his temper, but they have no explanation."

"The hall is guarded day and night," Deval added, "and there is no other way in or out. They couldn't go over the walls without anyone noticing."

"So the king issued a decree," Quentin said. "He will give the hand of one of his daughters to anyone who can solve the mystery."

"I take it others have tried," Alden said.

"Oh, yes," Khalil said. "Dozens upon dozens. Somehow the story has gotten out and whenever a young man new to town comes in, it's almost always someone who thinks he is going to solve the mystery, marry a princess, and become the next king."

Alden lifted his chin. "I see."

"Keeps me in business," Quentin said.

"Although you'd probably make even more if they stayed after giving up," Timicin said.

"Other than that," Deval said, "it's a really nice place. We do have some who come and stay, and very few leave."

"...and of those who do, most come back within a year," Gerasim said.

The door opened. A grizzled old man with short, scraggly hair and an equally short, scraggly beard entered. He carried a string of fish in one hand and cradled a ceramic tureen in the other.

"Jacob!" the men said at once.

Jacob held up the string.

"Dinner," Quentin said to Alden. Jacob walked toward Quentin and handed him the string and the tureen. Quentin disappeared through a door in the back of the room.

Jacob sat at the other side of the table from Alden. "New here?"

Alden nodded.

"Come to claim a princess?"

"No," Alden said softly.

"Smart man. Worthless, every single one of them. Not suitable marriage material."

Bennu turned in their direction and smiled. "But pretty. Every one of them."

"I don't know." Timicin took a swig of his mug of beer. "Pretty is good enough for many a man."

Khalil pointed at him. "Yes, your wife is pretty. But if it wasn't for her gift at the potter's wheel...."

"...and her talent for thrift," Deval added, holding up a finger.

"...you'd be a poor man indeed." Khalil smiled wryly.

Timicin inclined his head. "Can't argue with that."

"Exactly what I mean," Jacob said. "Don't know what I'd do without my Rose and her sewing. Those princesses don't know anything about life, locked away for years like that. Queen Beatrice managed her family's estate—everything from breeding the horses to instructing the cooks. King Reginald oversaw the repairs to the roads, bridges, sewers, and aqueducts. When they came to rule, they knew how regular folk live."

Quentin came out of the back and resumed his stance behind the counter. "Supper will be ready soon."

The men slapped the counter. "Good." "Can't wait."

Quentin turned to Alden. "You're in luck, my friend. Jacob catches the best-tasting fish from the river, and my wife makes a sumptuous fish stew."

"Magical fish," Bennu said.

Jacob waved a hand. "Aaaah," he said derisively. "Just fish and you know it."

"Alden hasn't heard the story," Khalil said.

"Who wants to tell it this time?" Quentin said.

"I told it to the last stranger who came in," Deval said. "Why don't you tell him, Quentin."

"Glad to." Quentin leaned comfortably against the counter and faced Alden. "Jacob isn't a believer, but most of us in this kingdom think that the river borders the land of the Enchanters."

"That's why the fish from there are so good," Bennu interjected.

Timicin nodded to Jacob. "And Jacob, there, is the only man who can go into the enchanted forest and fish from the Enchanted River without coming to grief."

"Aaaah, nonsense." Jacob waved a hand. "I keep telling you, anyone can go there."

"Anyone *can*," Quentin said, "but they tend to be laid up for a week with a hurt or an illness afterwards."

"All people need to do is watch what they're doing and where they're going," Jacob said.

Quentin continued, "It's not just the forest and the river. Strange things happen here. Objects appear and disappear."

"People lose and find things all the time," Jacob said. "Doesn't mean it's magic."

"They appear and disappear at very convenient times," Quentin said. "Folks get glimpses of tall, thin people with an aura about them."

"Moonlight and shadows."

"Most of all," Quentin said, "when my wife prepares the fish, the bones come right out and no one has ever choked on a bone."

"Matilda is a good cook, that's all."

Quentin straightened up and turned to Alden. "Speaking of food, making fish stew takes time. Why don't I show you around and find you a room."

Alden picked up his rucksack and nodded.

Quentin turned to the other men. "Watch the place while we're gone."

"We always do," Bennu said.

Quentin escorted Alden through a door in the back. "Since you're new here, you might find some of our ways different."

"I've been everywhere between the western and eastern seas. I've seen dozens of different ways of doing things."

Quentin smiled. "Even so. The Enchanters have been here longer than any of our forebears, or so the storytellers say, and though we don't see them anymore, they left behind some of their ways of doing things." He walked across a hallway and opened a door. "This is the washroom."

Alden stepped inside. A large wooden tub stood in the middle of the floor.

"If you want to wash, the water pump is here. The water is warm; if you want hot, just fill the kettle on the stove and light the fire. There's a plug at the bottom of the tub that goes into the drain."

Quentin walked into the hall again and opened another door. "This is the privy."

Alden looked inside. He saw something made of pottery, like a chamber pot, but shaped more like a chair, like a close stool. The base of the contrivance went all the way to the floor.

"Just sit or stand and do your business," Quentin said. "Then pull the chain. It will wash out the basin and open the drain."

"I wondered why there wasn't much of a smell."

Quentin motioned to a cabinet next to the contrivance. "Use the leaves, there, to wipe yourself. The little ones gather them from plants at the edge of the enchanted woods and sell them for slivers." Seeing Alden's puzzled expression, he added, "Our smallest coins." He nodded inside. "They keep the room smelling decent, too."

Quentin continued to another door which opened to another small room. "We wash up here."

Alden noticed a shelf with a row of pottery bowls, filled with water.

"If the bowls are empty," Quentin said, "fill the pitcher from the pump. Towels are hanging there, and there's soap next to the bowls."

Quentin continued down the hall to a flight of stairs. They ascended and walked through another hallway. He reached into a pocket and put a key in the lock of a door. After opening it, he handed the key to Alden. "Your room."

He stepped inside. A bed covered by a quilt dominated the room...not that the bed was large, but the room was small. A window with curtains was set in the wall to the right of the bed. Next to the bed was a cabinet with a washbowl. A small wardrobe stood to the side, and pegs for hanging clothes stood out from the wall. A chair and table stood under the windowsill.

Alden turned to Quentin. "Very nice. Thank you."

Quentin nodded. "Settle in. We'll call when supper's ready." He closed the door behind him.

Alden put his rucksack on the floor next to the table and sat in the chair. He took off his boots and sat back with a sigh. After a few moments, he bent down and examined the boots, finding a small hole in the sole of the left boot. That would have to be fixed, but for now, he reached into his rucksack and removed a leather patch. He put it inside the boot. That would cover the hole until he could get it repaired.

Standing, he took off his coat and hung it on a peg. Then he sat on the bed and lay down. A bed felt so good after uncounted days of sleeping on the ground.

"Alden! Supper!"

Alden awakened. It seemed as if he had only been in the bed for a few seconds. He went to the chair and put on his boots, then washed in the basin before leaving the room.

In the main room, Quentin remained behind the counter, with the four regulars still sitting there. Jacob sat at the table, his tureen at his elbow, and a bowl of stew in front of him. Opposite him on the table was another bowl of stew.

Quentin pointed. "That's yours, Alden. Need a beer to wash it down?"

"Yes, thank you." Alden sat. He took the spoon there and took his first taste. He looked up at Quentin as the tavern owner set a tankard of beer on the table. "Compliments to your wife. This is delicious."

Quentin smiled. "I'll tell her." He walked back to the counter.

Alden noticed Jacob having some trouble eating the stew. He took a clean spoon out of his pocket, wrapped in linen. He got up, walked near Jacob, and unwrapped the spoon. "Here, try this." He dipped the spoon in Jacob's bowl and moved the bowl of the spoon toward Jacob's mouth. Jacob closed his mouth around it.

"Better?" Alden asked.

Jacob nodded.

Alden handed him the spoon. "A lot of men in my units had bad teeth or mouth wounds. One of my fellow soldiers, a whittler, carved a special spoon that he said worked better. It was very popular."

Jacob took the spoon from this mouth and examined it. "Maybe I could make one of these."

"Jacob's a tinkerer," Gerasim said over Alden's shoulder. "He fixes things."

Alden looked up to see the others in the inn surrounding him.

"And makes things," Jacob added.

"Where did you say you got that?" Timicin asked Alden.

Alden straightened. "A fellow soldier. He carved them and gave them out. I didn't need one but he told me you never know what will happen next, and I accepted the few he offered me."

"I know someone who could use one," Gerasim said.

"Yes, not everyone has good teeth," Deval said.

"I only have a couple more," Alden said.

"Gentlemen," Quentin said. "Jacob will give it a try, and if he gets busy, Alden might want to go to the silversmith's or woodcarver's shops in the morning and see if they can make more. Good way to earn extra coin...I'm sure they'd split the profits."

"Sounds good to me," Jacob said.

Alden turned to Quentin. "If you direct me in the morning, I may well do that."

A woman's voice said, "Your suppers, gentlemen."

They all turned. On the counter were five tureens. "Time to bring supper home to the wives," Khalil said. The men grabbed the tureens, set payment on the counter, and after giving warm parting greetings to the others, left.

"Need to get ready for the supper crowd." Quentin returned to the counter. The woman, presumably Matilda, had disappeared again.

Alden sat back and ate in peace, as Jacob seemed intent on his supper as well. In his travels, Alden had stayed at inns where there were "regulars" who came in and were served early and presumed this was the case here.

When Jacob finished his stew, he took the tureen and stood.

"Give our regards to Rose," Quentin called after him.

"I will." Jacob turned to Alden. "Nice meeting you."

"Nice meeting you, too." Alden's bowl was also empty. He took his and Jacob's bowls and the tankard and walked to the counter.

Quentin smiled. "Guests can leave them there. We have help coming in that clear and serve tables."

Alden shrugged. "Well, I have time and nothing to fill it."

Quentin inclined his head toward the door. "I can extend you credit for work, if you want to help in the kitchen."

"Much obliged." Alden walked through the door and found a clean, well-organized kitchen. He set the bowls and tankard next to a large, metal tub set on a chest-high platform.

"You must be Alden. I heard the talk from in here."

Alden nodded. "You must be Matilda. Pleased to meet you."

"What can you do?"

"I've done just about everything. I can clean vegetables, wash dishes...."

She nodded to the wash bowl. "You can start by washing those, then."

The next hours were busy. The noise level throughout the inn rose, servers and helpers came in and out. Then, suddenly, everything went quiet again.

Quentin ducked in. "Doors are locked. Cleaning the main room."

Matilda nodded and waved.

Alden found himself washing dishes with Matilda next to him, drying and putting them away.

"By the way, is there a shoemaker nearby? I need to get my boot fixed."

"Just go out, turn left, and walk along the main road until you come to a sign with a shoe. That's them."

"Is there a place where I can change my coins?"

"Well, anyone will take a gold or silver coin by weight."

"So, you don't have your own coins?"

"We do. When we get coins from outsiders, we take them to the coin shop. They melt them and cast them into our own coins. You can take your coins there, too, if you want."

"Is there a woodcarver? Quentin said one might be able to carve my special spoons. He also mentioned a silversmith."

"I heard that," Matilda said. "Just about everyone's along the main street. Just keep walking until you see a sign. And by the way," she added, "I should tell you that Jacob may not be the one to make the spoons. He does fix things well enough, but not always to their original condition. When folks need their things fixed fast and working and cheap, they go to Jacob, but if they need things restored like new, they go to the tinkerer at the other end of town."

"I'll keep that in mind." Alden handed her another clean plate. "I saw that you gave the other men pots of stew to take home to their families. Do they do that all the time?"

"Jacob, yes, every day. Rose can cook, but her rheumatism bothers her these days. Jacob brings the stew home, sets the table, and sits with her as she eats. The others take home dinner once or twice a week as a favor to their wives. Not all of them can cook well, and the men don't all cook, either." She smiled. "Keeps us and the other taverns in business."

"Very much appreciated, I assume."

"Yes. They're men that appreciate their brides, not like some."

"Some?"

She leaned in his direction. "I shouldn't say, but all Trent the candlemaker does is sit in the shop and take the payments. His wife, Penelope, does the lion's share of the work, actually makes the candles. His name on the door, of course, not hers. Has to be that way. You know how people talk."

Alden lifted his chin. "I do."

"Of course I wouldn't say this to just anyone."

"You can rely on my discretion."

Matilda smiled. "I had a feeling about you, young man."

When they were done, they both walked into the main area of the tavern where Quentin was adjusting chairs behind tables. He turned to Alden. "Turning in?"

"I think I will, yes. Nice bed."

"It's a clear night outside. Take the ladder on the second floor and stand on the roof awhile. The stars are especially bright around here. Mind the basin; we collect rainwater."

"I will. Thank you."

Alden easily found the ladder at the end of the hall. He climbed up, opened the door, and crawled out onto the roof. Standing up, he saw that Quentin was right; the stars seemed exceptionally brilliant. Turning toward the mountains, he spotted the castle by the lights in the windows. He wondered what the princesses might be up to, and if it was knowable, if anything was knowable. Turning again, he saw the lights in the town. Lamplighters had done their work and he could see the streets clearly, as well as the shops. People walked or strolled along the streets. A man sauntered along playing a pleasant tune on a lute, accompanied by a youngster with a large cup. Occasional passersby dropped in coins.

He turned toward the forest. At first, it appeared the same as any other forest he had known, but as he continued to look at it, he spotted what seemed to be a shimmering...which was moving. He walked to the edge of the roof to get a closer view. This could be a line of people, walking in single file, bearing lanterns...but no, he had seen such lines many times in his life, and this was not the same, somehow. As he watched, the shimmering seemed to move to the range of hills bordering the forest. Then it faded.

Alden scratched his chin. Enchanters? He squared his shoulders and took a long breath. Whatever it was, it seemed harmless and had nothing to do with him. He knew from hard experience that investigating things that were not his businesses had unfortunate results more often than not. Taking another long breath, he went back inside and then to bed.

Chapter 3

Alden dreamed of entering the inn, but this time it was empty except for a tall, thin man behind the counter. His clothes were elegant without being grandiose. His face wore a pleasant expression, but he did not smile. He turned to Alden, though he did not speak immediately.

Alden set his rucksack on the floor and met the man's gaze.

"I have been waiting for you," he said softly.

Not having an answer to that, Alden simply continued to look at him.

The man took out a clean rag and wiped the counter, though it was neither dirty nor wet. "You have work to do," he added.

"What sort of work?" Alden asked.

"You will know when you see it," the man said.

Bells rang. Alden looked up and around to see where they came from...

...and woke up.

The bells continued to ring. He also heard a call to prayer. It reminded him of the large trading cities he had visited, such as Constantinople, where people of a number of religious beliefs lived and worked.

He pulled the covers back and sat up, feeling well-rested. The entire night had passed without a nightmare or ill feeling. He had found his place of peace at last.

After relieving himself, washing, and dressing, he made his way downstairs to the main room. Matilda held the door to the street open, allowing workers to bring in baskets of vegetables, eggs, and cheese, as well as bags of flour. Others brought in large metal containers that sloshed. From the white drippings on the outside, he guessed those contained milk.

"Morning, Alden, how did you sleep?" Quentin called behind him.

He turned to see Quentin at the back. "Very well, thank you," he answered.

"Have a seat at the counter and I'll bring you breakfast." Quentin came out quickly with a plate of thick warm bread, butter, and cheese. "Cider or beer?" he asked.

"Cider," Alden said.

Quentin nodded and returned with a mug. After setting it down, he disappeared into the back.

By the time Alden had finished eating, Matilda had conveyed the morning delivery into the kitchen. Quentin reappeared with a young woman. "This is Alden, Signe," he said to her. "He's new."

Alden stood and nodded. "Pleased to meet you."

Signe nodded in turn. "Pleased to meet you, too." She turned back to Quentin. "Until later, then." She disappeared into the back. Moments later, Alden heard the back door open and shut.

Quentin turned to Alden. "Our brewer. Her sister, Ceily, is our vintner. We have the best beer and wine around town. Of course, we keep our sources a secret. You know how people talk."

"I do."

Alden felt his first stop in the city should be the coin exchange. Following Matilda's direction to follow the city street until he saw a sign, he strolled down the walkway. The walks were not crowded, but he saw a constant stream of people in both directions. The clothing styles varied. Some wore clothing he had largely seen in the East, some wore clothing he usually saw in the Holy Land, some wore clothing that came from the far south, other clothing reminded him of home. Apparently people from all over the continent found rest here.

He saw a wooden sign protruding from a building with pictures of coins painted on it. The building had a door, but his attention was drawn to a large opening in the side with a counter. Shutters set back indicated the opening was closed at night.

Inside, sitting at the counter, was a woman about his age. She wore a simple cap on her head. Long straight black hair streamed out from under it in the back. Her dress was plain, a simple faded pink color. She had an oval face, and large gray eyes. He found her attractive and wondered if she were married.

Alden stood aside while the woman counted coins into the hand of a man with two youngsters clinging to his pants. When they stepped away, Alden came forward.

He smiled and put his coins on the counter. "I'd like to exchange these for local ones, if I could."

She looked up at him with a weary expression. "You're new here?"

"Just came in yesterday."

She sighed and looked down at the coins. "I suppose you're here to marry a princess."

"No. I never even heard of princesses here until after I arrived."

She looked up at him again. "Now that you've heard, I suppose you're going to try to solve the mystery?"

He shook his head. "Where I'm from, and elsewhere, it's common for marriages to be arranged. But that's not for me. I'm not interested in a woman given to me as a prize. I'd rather that my bride feel something for me first, and I for her."

She examined his face with what seemed to be interest. "What did bring you here?"

"Rest. Peace."

She turned to the coins again. "You may have found the right place. We're not perfect, but we generally get along here." She reached underneath the counter and brought out a scale. "I'll weigh your coins and give you the equivalent."

"Much obliged." As she weighed them, he said, "Do you melt them down?"

She gestured behind her. "No, the brothers do. They're good at metalwork, not so good at keeping records."

"Married to one of them?"

She chuckled heartily. "No. I'm unmarried."

"At your age, I'm surprised," Alden blurted out. He hoped he had not been too bold.

She looked up and smiled at him. "Like you, I think couples should choose each other. I haven't found my choice yet." She continued her weighing. When she finished, she counted coins to him and explained what each was worth. "We keep a small commission for exchanging coins," she added.

He nodded. "As expected." He took the coins and pocketed them. "I hope we meet again sometime. I'm Alden."

"Philippa," she said amicably. "I expect you'll be here again. We have many regulars. People who accumulate small coins want to exchange for larger ones, or have large ones and want to exchange for smaller ones...."

"I'll remember," he said, and seeing others waiting out of the corner of his eye, stepped aside.

His plan was to go to the shoemaker next. Again, he walked until he saw a wooden sign with shoes painted on it. The shop door was open. Walking in, he saw a broad-chested man sitting in a chair examining a large basket full of shoes next to his feet.

He looked up and smiled at Alden. "May I help you?"

Alden leaned down and tapped his left boot. "I have a hole in my boot. Can you fix it?"

The man turned and called, "Li!"

A woman entered from an open door in the back of the room.

The man turned back to Alden. "Take off your boot." He gestured at Li. "Man has a hole in his boot."

Alden had the boot off.

Li reached for it. "Let me see." She held it by the top and turned it to examine the sole. Nodding, she said, "Yes, I can fix this. Have a seat." She disappeared through the door in the back.

Alden looked around and saw several empty chairs. He sat.

The man turned to him. "Li does the boots. I do the shoes."

Alden nodded.

"I'm Jin. You're new, I take it?"

"Yes. Alden. Just came in yesterday."

"Li and I came in seven years ago. Heard about this place from a customer traveling through and stopping in my father's shop to buy shoes. Difficult to find."

"Difficult for me, too, but I kept walking because I had nowhere else to go."

He nodded. "Same. Too many determined people following us."

"Trouble? If you don't mind my asking, that is."

"Not at all. Her family thought I wasn't good enough for her. My family thought she wasn't good enough for me. We married anyway and thought that settled the matter. Instead, it made a lot of people angry."

"Enough to chase you?"

"Unbelievable, isn't it?"

"Not to me. I've seen it happen, about everywhere I've been."

He nodded. "When we came in, with our shoemaking tools and little else, people asked us what brought us here, and when we told them, they immediately took us to heart." He leaned toward Alden and added in a low, conspiratorial voice, "Seems we aren't the only ones." He leaned back again in the chair with a smile.

Alden smiled back, then gestured to the basket. "Someone seems to have brought in a lot of shoes for repair."

Jin reached into the basket and took out a shoe by the heel. It almost fell apart in his hand. "These are beyond repair. Has anyone told you about the princesses yet?"

Alden nodded.

"These are this morning's haul. They were new yesterday. We keep the scraps for repairing other shoes and for parts for making new shoes." He returned the shoe in his hand to the basket and gestured to the shelves of shoes on the wall. "I sent off another twelve pairs with the messenger this morning when he brought these in. I can't complain. It keeps me in business. The palace pays well. I can't help but wonder how they get this way, though."

"Any reports from those who tried to find out?"

He shrugged. "The young men who have offered to solve the riddle have mysteriously fallen asleep keeping watch and can't be roused until morning. Or they go into the forest and twist an ankle. Or they try to make a clever trap that doesn't work. They've all tried what they claimed to be clever ways to spy on the princesses. None have succeeded yet."

"As a shoemaker, do you have any guesses as to how the shoes get this way?"

Jin glanced toward the basket again. "The only time I've seen anything like this is when I was apprenticed at my father's shop and there was a dance troupe performing in the city. I happened to see one of the performances. Vigorous and beautiful, but they could wear out a pair of shoes in a night. Sometimes more than one pair. My father was always happy when they came to town because we made a lot of money. But who could the princesses be dancing with?" He spread his hands. "No one could get in or out of that section of the castle. It's locked and the walls are guarded."

"Maybe they dance by themselves?"

"The walled garden is observed all night. Empty. If they were dancing in their rooms, there would be sounds on the floorboards. It's completely quiet, or so the reports say."

Alden rubbed his chin. "If it's ever found out, it'll probably be something no one could have imagined."

As they were talking, there were sounds of working in the next room. Now the sounds stopped. Li emerged through the door with Alden's boot. "It's fixed."

Alden stood. She handed him the boot. He turned it over and smiled. "Thank you. This is good work."

She smiled. "Thank you."

Alden brought out a handful of coins. "How much do I owe you?"

"A leaf and a couple of slivers," Jin said.

Alden looked at the coins. He found a medium-sized coin with a leaf impressed on it. He gave that to Jin plus two of the smallest coins.

Li and Jin nodded. "Thank you and come again."

Alden put the coins away and put his boot back on. "I'd be happy to."

The next place Alden visited was the silversmith's. He looked into the window at the display and saw various forks, spoons, plates, kettles, and other metal items. He went in and showed the wooden spoon to the proprietor, Vasily.

The silversmith examined the spoon and nodded. "I've tried various forms myself, but this is a shape I hadn't thought of."

"Can you make it in metal?"

He rubbed his chin. "I think I can. It would work much better in metal than in wood. I would think that a wooden spoon this thin wouldn't last very long."

"My friend carved a lot of them for that very reason, though he tried hardwood whenever he could."

"Is your friend around to ask which wood he used?"

"He was a fellow soldier. I'm sad to say that whatever skills he had were buried with him."

Vasily looked at Alden sympathetically. "Sorry. A lot of talent is wasted in war. I'm glad we don't have those here."

"So I was given to understand."

Vasily held up the spoon. "Come back in three days. I may have something to show you then."

"Thank you."

Having no other place to be, Alden strolled down the street just to get more acquainted with the city. He found what appeared to be a city square, with a large fountain in the middle. Stone benches stood here and there surrounding the fountain. People in small groups sat or stood and talked. Others walked up to the fountain and dipped containers into the water and carried them away.

Not far from the fountain, Alden saw what seemed to be an open-air carpenter's shop. Curious, he went over and looked in. He saw Jacob bending over a wooden chair.

"Be with you in a minute," Jacob said without looking up.

"Just saying hello," Alden replied.

Jacob straightened, faced Alden, and smiled. "Oh. Hello. Haven't gotten to your spoon yet, young man. I'm fixing Sister Angelica's chair."

"There's no need to hurry. I just wanted to see the shop."

Jacob gestured at the shelves and workbenches. The tools and materials were scattered here and there, but Alden could see they were arranged in rough groupings. "It may not be pretty, but I know where everything is."

"As it should be," Alden said.

"Why don't I bring you in the house to meet Rose," Jacob said. "She's always happy for company, and you can stay and share the midday meal."

"That would be nice. Thank you."

Jacob walked to the back of the shop and opened the door.

When Alden reached the other side, he saw a small but well-kept home with a bed in a corner, a kitchen and hearth on the other side, and an area with a rug surrounded by chairs. In one of the chairs sat a gray-haired woman, sewing by the light coming in through a window. She looked up at Alden.

"This is Alden, Rose, the man I told you about last night."

Rose nodded. "Come in and sit."

"Thank you. I will." Alden took a chair facing her.

Jacob went back through the door to the shop and shut it behind him.

"I understand that you're new here." She continued to sew as she talked.

"Yes, ma'am. Just arrived yesterday."

"Call me Rose."

"Rose."

"You'll fit in here just fine, Alden. The Enchanters are particular about who they let in."

"Have you spoken to them?" he asked curiously.

She laughed briefly, and kindly. "No, no one living has ever seen one. There are written accounts and stories. You should come to the city square on Sunday afternoon and listen to the storytellers. They recite the history every week. The children never tire of it, and some of the older folks, too."

"I'll do that. Thank you."

"Do you have work?"

"For now, I'm helping out at Quentin and Matilda's inn."

She nodded. "Good folk. If you ever want something different, Jacob could use a hand...not that he'd admit it."

"I don't know much about carpentry beyond some very simple fixes."

"That's all right. Jacob can teach you. He's slowing down, not that he'd admit that, either. Folks around here have been kind about it, but they've noticed, too."

"I'll think it over."

"I'm slowing down myself. My hands aren't what they were, and my legs are almost useless."

He looked over at her hands as she continued sewing a patch on the knee of a pair of pants. "I wouldn't have been able to tell unless you told me."

She smiled. "I've been doing this almost my whole life. I guess I'm still better than anyone who couldn't sew, or sewed only a little, but I've noticed the difference."

"Are those Jacob's pants?"

"Oh, no. I mend and sew for others. Brings in enough money so I can buy some frills from time to time." She gestured to one of the walls. He turned and saw a couple of crates piled with clothes next to a sturdy table holding cloth, thread, and scissors. "I sew mostly nightgowns for ladies and clothes for children, but I sew a little for men, too." She nodded toward the crates. "Since you're going to be staying here, if you need something else, go ahead and look through the bins."

He walked over and started to sort through the clothes, carefully removing the ones on top and setting them on the table as he searched. He intended to return them to the crate when he finished browsing. An embroidered shirt caught his eye. He removed it and the matching jacket under it and the pants under that.

Holding them up, he said, "This is very good work. You could wear this to court."

Rose laughed cheerily. "Thank you, but that's more of a church or festival outfit."

"This would pass for court clothing where I come from."

"Oh, I guess you could wear it if the king or queen summoned you. But if you wanted to go to a court dance or celebration, I would go to Juno's shop, across the way and down the street. She does some embroidery for me and we split the cost, but she's the one that sews outfits for the royalty and court officers."

He held the pieces against his body and estimated that they would fit him. "How much for the three?"

"A couple of leafs would do."

He put the clothes on the table back into the crate and kept the ones he intended to purchase.

"There's paper and twine next to the table to wrap it."

"Thanks." Once his purchase was wrapped, he returned to the chair and set two coins on the small table next to her chair before sitting again.

"Thank you," she said. "If you need your clothes washed, the washerwoman is within sight of the city square."

"I'll keep that in mind, thanks. It's always nice to have fresh clothes."

"If you're serious about going to a royal ball, there is one coming up. Anyone who dresses right can go. Most folks stay home, though a crowd lines up outside the palace to watch those going in. Juno and Raven would be happy to outfit you."

"Raven is Juno's daughter?"

She shook her head. "Hearthmate, actually, and her partner in the shop. She does more than her share of the sewing and embroidery. They work well together. Raven doesn't live there, in the rooms behind the shop, though. We think she has folks to take care of and needs to go home in the evening to tend to them. Families need to do what they have to do. We try not to pry to preserve their dignity. You know how people talk."

"I do."

"Since you plan to stay...." She looked straight at him. "You do plan to stay?"

"Without a doubt. I have nowhere else to go."

She nodded. "That's a common story around here. If you're staying, you might think about getting a place for yourself. Homes are hard to come by. Very few ever leave—permanently, that is—and some new folks come in every year. Then of course, the folks that are born here grow up. There's usually a house raising party. That's how Jacob and I got this house when we married. But sometimes there's a vacancy. Folks die without issue, sadly, or someone moves away."

"Any sleeping in the streets?"

"We try to take care of our own here. The boarding houses take in poorer folks, and the Sisters of Charity take in older folks and those without family."

A bell rang outside. Rose set her sewing on the table next to her. "I'd best get started on the midday meal." She put her hands firmly on the arms of the chair. He rushed toward her to help her to her feet.

Once standing, she smiled at him. "Thank you, young man."

"Can I help with the meal?"

She nodded. "I'll show you."

By the time Jacob came through the door, the table was set for three and a bowl of grapes, apples, and pears had been placed in the middle of the table, along with bread, butter, and cheese. Alden had set out the cups and filled them with cider.

Mealtime conversation largely consisted of Jacob and Rose telling Alden about the local merchants and where to find them, as well as the location of various city landmarks. By the time they finished, Alden had a basic idea of the city's offerings.

As they were cleaning up, there was a knock at the door Jacob had come through.

"Jacob?" a woman's voice called.

"Be right there, Sister Angelica."

Alden turned to Rose with a questioning look, and she nodded to indicate she did not need any more help at the moment. "Thank you for the meal, it was very good," Alden said. He picked up his package, then followed Jacob out the door and closed it behind him.

"Your chair's fixed, Sister Angelica." Jacob led her to the chair and indicated the repairs with a gesture.

She examined the chair, nodded, and produced coins from a pocket. "Very good, as usual, Jacob. I know I can always count on you."

Jacob accepted the coins. "Glad to be of service." He turned to Alden. "This is Alden, Sister Angelica. Just came in yesterday."

She smiled and nodded at him. "Pleased to meet you."

"Pleased to meet you, too, Sister Angelica."

She grasped the chair.

"Let me carry it for you," Alden offered.

She let go. "Why, thank you, Alden."

Alden tucked his package of clothing under an arm, picked up the chair, and turned back to Jacob. "Thank you for your hospitality."

"Always glad to have company. Say, do you want to come back here later and go fishing with me?"

"Not today," Alden said politely. "But I'll remember that you asked."

Jacob nodded. "I'll get to your spoon later."

"There's no need to hurry on my account," Alden said. "I know you need to attend to paying customers first." He turned to Sister Angelica. She began walking and he followed.

"Jacob does good work," she said once they were a distance from the shop. "Everything comes back sturdy, though the fixes aren't always pretty. I take it you noticed?"

Alden turned the chair he was carrying. A thick piece of wood had been nailed over a break in the chair leg to join the two parts together again. "Yes, I can see what you mean."

"We keep an eye on Rose and Jacob. They're getting along in years, and not as spry as they used to be."

"So I am given to understand."

With a slight shake of the head, she added, "Tragic, what has happened to them in their lives. Their first child was stillborn. The second died in infancy. The third was killed by a runaway horse before his ninth birthday. They have no close family."

He took a breath. "I take it that the peace doesn't prevent illness and loss."

"Indeed it doesn't, sorry to say. But there are bright spots, too. You might want to come back to the city square on Sunday."

"Rose told me about the storytellers."

She nodded. "There is that. There is also dancing, and singing, and music. It's a good place to meet people. A young man might find a maiden catching his eye."

He grinned. "Are you a matchmaker, Sister Angelica?"

She smiled wryly. "We do what we can for the increase of happiness."

"I am all in favor of that, Sister Angelica."

Chapter 4

Sister Angelica's convent seemed to be in a religious district. As they approached, Alden could identify two churches, a synagogue, a mosque, a Hindu temple, and a Buddhist temple. Other buildings could have been houses of worship for other beliefs.

Alden was not invited into the convent and did not expect to be. At the door, Sister Angelica handed the chair to another member of her order and gestured for Alden to follow. She led him to a large square two-story building with a courtyard in the middle. It reminded him of Spanish architecture.

"This is our housing for the poor and elderly. Families have several rooms together, singles have one room each. The building is administered by our religious community."

Alden nodded. "You work together."

She smiled. "Oh, yes. There's not enough of us to support this singly. It's the same with the hospital. We have physicians of several traditions. Frankly, I think it's improved the care."

A woman stepped in the courtyard and gestured to Sister Angelica.

She waved back and turned to Alden. "Duty calls. Thank you for your help. Can you find your way back?"

"I think I can. Thank you."

Once back on the main street, Alden strolled in the direction of Quentin and Matilda's inn. He stopped briefly at Timicin's pottery shop. Timicin introduced Alden to his wife, Tuya, before they became busy with customers. As he went on, he saw Gerasim and another man in front of an undertaker's building loading a coffin into a horse-drawn wagon, but did not interrupt them in their solemn work.

Seeing the horse reminded Alden to look around and note again how clean the streets were. Peering down the lane, he spotted a street sweeper at work, picking up debris and placing it in a two-wheeled handcart.

As he neared the city square, he spotted Juno and Raven's shop. The door was open; he stepped inside. Both women looked up as he entered. One sat near the shop window, embroidering. The other knelt near a dress that had been placed over a form. He introduced himself and found that the embroiderer was Raven and the dressmaker was Juno.

"I heard that there was a ball coming up at the palace. I wondered if you could make me an outfit."

Juno looked up at him skeptically. "That will cost you a branch, at least."

Alden opened his purse and looked through the coins. He had a couple of larger gold coins with branches impressed on them. Taking one out, he extended it to Juno. "Will this do as a start?"

Juno stood and took it. "It will." She smiled. "I'll need to measure you, and then you can look over the sketches and cloth pieces and see what styles interest you."

"I'll trust you to make something appropriate."

Her smile grew wider. "Even so. Customers who say that have ended up dissatisfied in the past. We aim to please on the first time."

"Very well."

As Juno measured him, Raven kept embroidering. Without looking up, she said, "Are you seeking the hand of a princess?"

"I admit that I'm curious, but no. I'm more interested in the dancing."

This time Raven did look up. "You're a dancer?"

"I don't earn my bread that way, but I grew up in an estate, and dancing made the long cold winter nights more bearable. My mother always said that dancing could dispel any gloom."

Raven smiled. "It can indeed."

"In my travels, soldiering, there was little to do at night except dance, sing, and tell stories. I learned more dances from the men I was with."

"If you dance well," Raven said, "the king and queen will call you to the thrones and pair you with a princess. They give these balls so that the princesses will have a chaperoned event to meet prospective marriage partners."

"You won't really see any of the princesses, though," Juno added. "The princesses either wear a mask or put ointments and salves on their faces, as we heard Queen Elizabeth of England did."

"So you get news from outside," Alden said, trying not to bend too much so Juno could keep measuring.

"The merchant's guild sends a delegation to the closest cities once a month to trade," Juno said. "They bring news."

"And there's a board on the city square to post the newspaper," Raven said.

"Word gets around pretty fast, mostly through the Sunday gatherings in the city square." Juno finished measuring and motioned Alden to a table with cloth samples and sketches of clothing.

As Juno showed the sketches and samples, Alden pointed and nodded to ones that he favored. Once he had settled on a style, he picked up his package, which he had set on a chair while Juno measured him.

"The ball is three weeks away," Juno said. "Can you come for a fitting in say, five days?"

"Yes. I know good clothing takes time."

"It's not only that," Raven said. "The princesses wear out their gowns as well as their shoes, though not as quickly. We're constantly sewing more."

"I wonder what the king and queen think about all that expense...the shoes and gowns and all."

"Oh, they can afford it," Juno said. "It's the mystery that annoys them."

"And it's not a topic of conversation very much of the time... well, when the whole affair started, there were flares of temper, but things settled down once it became a regular happening," Raven said. "The princesses eat their morning and evening meals with their parents, and it's usually very cordial. The king begins every meal by asking if they're ready to tell him what is happening, they're silent for a moment, and then a different conversation continues."

"How do you know all this?" Alden asked, curious.

"I deliver the gowns to the palace regularly," Juno said. "The maids and cooks and attendants speak freely."

Alden smiled. "Yes, I know how people talk."

After leaving the clothier's, he made his way back to the shoe shop. Again, the door was open. When he walked in, he saw Jin hard at work on a shoe form, sewing the body of a shoe to the sole.

Jin looked up and smiled in recognition. "Did you find a hole in your other boot?"

Alden smiled back. "No, though if I did, this is the place I would come. I heard there's dancing on Sunday in the city square, and that there's a ball coming up. I need dancing shoes."

Jin straightened up. "Those I am an expert in making!" He gestured to a chair. "Have a seat and take off your boots so I can measure your feet."

Alden did so.

Jin came over with a measuring tape and knelt. "As long as I'm measuring your feet, you might also want to order some shoes for everyday wear. Save some wear and tear on the boots and will cost you only a couple of leafs more."

Alden nodded. "Good idea. I'll do that."

By the time he returned to the inn, the regulars were already there.

Khalil gestured to Alden's package. "Been shopping?"

"Yes, I bought an outfit from Rose."

"She makes good, sturdy clothes, especially for children," Bennu said.

"So I understand."

"By the time you take your package upstairs, Jacob will probably arrive with the fish," Quentin said.

Alden took his time, going to his room, opening the package, and putting the clothes away. By the time he returned to the main room, he saw Jacob sitting in the same chair as he had the night before.

Alden sat across from him.

Jacob took out a metal spoon, which appeared to have been hammered, and set it on the table. "I did my best, but I don't think it works as good as the wooden one. You might want to ask Vasily, the silversmith, if he could make one."

Alden raised his head and took a long breath. "Good idea. I think I will do that."

* * *

The next morning, after helping Quentin and Signe move beer barrels in the cellar, Quentin approached Alden. Handing him a purse, he said, "Would you be willing to go to the coin exchange and trade these for me? Philippa will know what I want."

Alden took the purse. "I'd be happy to." His tone was completely sincere, since he had been thinking of how he might make up an excuse to see Philippa again.

At the coin exchange, Alden found himself waiting as Philippa changed coins for an older woman. As Philippa counted the coins on the counter, she glanced in Alden's direction, and threw him a look of what he hoped was pleasant surprise.

He stepped forward with a smile when it was his turn. "Quentin asked me to bring these to you for an exchange. He said you would know what to do."

She took the offered purse and opened it. "Yes. Quentin is a regular customer."

As she weighed the coins on the scale, she added, "Quentin must have confidence in you to give you such an errand."

He nodded. "I'm honored by his trust."

She favored him with a wry smile. "Is it well-founded?"

"My father used to say that if a man has no honor, he has nothing."

"Your father was a wise man."

"Yes, though I regret to say I didn't appreciate how wise he was until I grew up and was out in the world."

"That seems to be the case with fathers and sons."

When she finished weighing, she brought out newly minted coins and placed them in the purse.

As she handed the purse back to him, he said, "What do you do for your midday meal?"

She paused for a moment before answering. "The shop is closed for an hour. Food vendors set up around city square."

"May I meet you there and purchase your repast? I have plenty of my own coin, still."

She smiled kindly. "You may." She nodded to the next customer in line.

Alden arrived at the city square before the midday bell. He sat on a stone bench and waited. As Philippa had predicted, various food vendors arrived, set up tables, and spread their wares. He saw Philippa walking in his direction and rose to meet her. When they were face to face, he bowed slightly.

She nodded and smiled. "And what do you like to eat?"

"I'm new here. You make the selection."

She gestured to a table. "The sausages are good. As is the roast chicken," she added, indicating another table.

"Either is fine with me. Or both."

She led the way to the table with the roast chicken. The vendor sliced a serving and put it in the napkin she had spread in her hand. Quentin had coached Alden as to what to do; he had a napkin, as well.

Alden paid the vendor and Philippa stepped to the next table, taking slices of apple. Again, Alden took slices of his own and paid. Then they stopped at a cider vendor. Philippa produced a ceramic cup, and Alden brought out his slightly battered tin cup, paying before the vendor poured in the cider. Philippa sat with her food in hand at a nearby stone bench. He sat next to her.

They ate companionably, silently at first. He noticed that she handled the food delicately, taking small bites and wiping her fingers on the edge of her napkin. He noted her stealing glances at him, as if noting his table manners in turn. In that he had nothing to be ashamed of, having been gently brought up, though in the field, he was less fastidious.

"How do you like it here so far?" she asked.

"Very much," he said. "I haven't slept this well since I was a boy. It's peaceful here."

"Were you raised in the country?"

"My father was an estate holder. I was the youngest among seven brothers."

"Any sisters?"

"Two."

She nodded. "I come from a large family, as well."

Something blocked the sun. Both looked up. Jacob stood over them. He extended his hand, showing coins settled in his palm.

"Philippa, Rose has a customer and can't make change. Can you change some coins for us?"

Philippa spoke kindly but firmly. "Jacob, we've talked about this. My midday meal is my time. You can come to the shop

when it opens again. Or Rose can give a note of credit instead
of change and the customer can take it to the shop."

"But you're right here."

Meanwhile, Alden brought out his purse and opened it. "I
can make change for you, Jacob." They exchanged coins and
Jacob left.

Philippa turned to Alden. "You learned the coin values
quickly."

He smiled at her. "I had a good teacher."

She smiled back. "Thank you." The smile faded slightly. "You
shouldn't let Jacob take advantage of you like that, though. He
is more than bold in asking for favors."

"It's no trouble. Besides, I may need to ask him for a favor
one day."

When they finished eating, Alden escorted Philippa back
to the coin exchange. Once she was inside the building, Alden
walked directly back to Jacob's shop.

Jacob was working on a table. "Be with you in a minute."

"I wondered if I could go in and see Rose."

Jacob looked up and nodded. "Her customer left." He returned
to hammering.

Alden knocked on the door to the house and went in when
Rose called.

"Nice to see you again," she said when he closed the door
behind him. "Have a seat. Do you need more clothes?"

"Not at the moment. I wanted to ask you about Philippa."

She smiled. "Oh, you know her?"

"I'm hoping to know her better."

The smile turned into a grin. "I see."

He smiled back. "I understand that she has an arrangement
with you to give a note of credit if you don't have change, and
the customer can take it and bring it to her, and she will take
the note and give them coins."

Rose nodded. "We settle accounts once a week. She comes
here and we go over the notes."

"That's very nice of her."

"Oh, it's not just me. She has the same arrangement with a
lot of the small merchants."

"The banks won't extend credit?"

She inclined her head briefly. "Most folks think that the banks are for only the large merchants. The bankers say this isn't so, but Philippa and the brothers at the coin exchange will handle amounts the bankers consider too small to bother with. The children with their slivers, for instance. And the bankers prefer that you go to them for exchanges. Philippa will come here."

"Sounds like a very practical system."

"Yes, we're happy with it." She took a breath. "But why not ask Philippa yourself? She would tell you."

He shrugged. "At the time, Philippa seemed to be annoyed at having her lunch interrupted, and I felt it was best not to ply her with questions when she was feeling that way."

"You'll make someone an excellent husband, Alden."

"I'm glad you think so. I hope your opinion will be shared by others."

On his way out, Alden again paused to talk to Jacob. "Is your invitation to go fishing with you still open?"

"Yes! Come by at 5 of the clock when I close shop."

Alden wore his traveling clothes and boots when he went to meet Jacob that afternoon. He helped Jacob close and lock the large doors.

Jacob had what seemed to be a purse hung at his belt. He held a chain with hooks and a net. "The fish bite good. You'll see." He led the way behind his shop. The forest edge was only a few furlongs outside the city. Alden could see a well-worn dirt path—more like a rut, really—that wound into the forest.

Turning, Jacob said, "Watch your step. The path is uneven." He turned back and kept walking.

Though the forest was large, with tall leafy trees, more than enough sunlight spilled through to illuminate the path. Still, Alden found himself tripping and catching himself at times, and once a branch slapped him in the face. He could understand why others might turn an ankle or take a fall here. Jacob, on the other hand, strode forward confidently, as if he knew the path well.

They stopped at the rocky bank of a stream, maybe as wide as a cart. In mid-stream, clear water flowed over stones and wound around a bend. Nearer the bank, the water formed a calmer pool.

Alden stopped at the water's edge and looked in. "Seems to be fairly shallow."

"The depth varies." Jacob put down his hooks, net, and fishing pole.

Alden reached into a pocket. "I brought a fishing line and hook."

Jacob turned to him. "The fishing's good here. Watch." He reached into his bag. When he took his hand out, he spread his fingers to show Alden. "Bread crumbs." He threw them out over the water.

Immediately, the water boiled with fish.

Alden hesitated a moment, surprised, and then threw in his line. At the same time, Jacob held his chain with one hand and threw in the part with the hooks.

Feeling a tug right away, Alden pulled in his line and landed a fish. He put it on the bank and stepped toward Jacob, helping him pull in the chain. Most of the hooks had a fish dangling from it. Jacob used the net to snag the fish that seemed about to drop from the hooks.

Alden surveyed the catch. He saw fish that resembled the Balkhash perch, gold with gray stripes, and fish that resembled the stone loach with its shiny scales. All were of adequate size for cooking and cleaning. "We seem to have more than enough for Matilda's fish stew."

Jacob smiled. "I told you it was easy."

"This is a lot of fish to take back," Alden said. "I could take off my shirt and we could pile them there, I suppose."

Jacob pointed. "Or we could use that basket."

Alden turned. A round, shallow basket rested between a nearby tree and the bank.

"Enchanter gift," Jacob said.

"Hm?"

"That's what we call them. Enchanter gifts. Things that appear when you need them. Especially in the forest, here. Folks more or less agree that anything found in the forest is for anyone to take." He waved at it. "Go ahead, Alden, grab it."

Alden reached for the basket. Jacob unhooked the fish that were still on the chain. Soon, all the fish were in the basket.

Alden hefted it. Jacob folded his chain. Alden let Jacob lead the way and carefully followed him back to the city, where Jacob stopped at his house and took the soup tureen before going to Quentin and Matilda's.

Sunday, Alden put on the pants, shirt, and jacket that Rose had sewn and the dancing shoes that Jin had constructed for him. He walked to the Protestant church that he had located in the city earlier. The service was familiar, and the preacher gave a sermon about the limitless love of God. After the service, he filed out with the rest of the congregation, and made the acquaintance of the parishioners in front of him and behind him. They all seemed to have heard of the stranger who was staying at Quentin and Matilda's inn.

After shaking the hand of the preacher at the church entrance, he followed the crowd to the city square. Food vendors had already set up. In addition, he saw musicians tuning their instruments here and there around the fountain.

"I was hoping to catch you," Vasily said, approaching him.

"Good to see you."

"Good to see you, too." He held out a spoon. "Here."

Alden took the spoon and examined it. "This is excellent work."

"It's an excellent spoon. I've already sold some in my shop." He reached into a pocket and brought out coins. "I think you deserve a share of the price."

Alden took the offered coins and pocketed them. "Thank you."

He nodded at Alden. "Keep the spoon, too."

"Thank you again."

"I need to get to my family. Linger awhile. You'll find plenty of things to see and do."

"I intend to."

After Vasily walked away, Alden looked around. He spied Philippa at a sausage vendor and ambled over. "Here, let me pay for that," he said, meeting her eye with a smile.

She smiled back. "Thank you."

Alden paid the vendor. "The rest is for a few sausages for me."

The vendor nodded and handed over a portion for Alden.

They bought a few other delicacies before walking to a stone bench to sit. This time they shared the bench with several others and were surrounded by even more people. As they ate, some of the musicians struck up a tune, and a number of people near them started to dance. Alden noticed that Philippa's attention was drawn to the dancers. He watched them with interest. The music and the dance reminded him of performances he had gone to in India. He admired their technique.

When the notes died away, Philippa turned to Alden. "Do you dance?"

"I do."

She wiped her fingers on her napkin, pocketed it, and stood. "Care to put it to the test?"

He pocketed his own napkin and rose to meet her. "I accept the challenge."

She smiled and walked toward another group of musicians. They had already started to play and had gathered perhaps a dozen people dancing to their tune, singly or in couples. Philippa led Alden to a small clearing on the square near the musicians and faced him. He bowed. She curtsied. She gathered her skirts and started with a basic step-close, step-close swaying movement, which he mirrored easily. As the music became move lively, she pulled up her skirts to about mid-calf and added kicking motions. Again, he matched her movements. Smiling approvingly, she dropped her skirts and raised a hand. Recognizing the cue, he moved closer and placed his palm against hers as they circled each other. Then, taking the lead, he guided her to more complex moves by the touch of his hand on hers or by placing an arm around her waist or shoulder. She gave him a slight nod and kept her eyes on his—and he on hers—as they moved along.

At some point, Alden became aware that the onlookers were clapping in rhythm and noted out of the corner of his eye that he and Philippa were the only dancers moving. But the music continued, and so did they.

Alden let Philippa go at the end of the last note and stood in place for a moment while he and she caught their breaths. The onlookers applauded. They waved acknowledgement.

"You are a magnificent dancer, sir," she said to him with a wide smile.

He bowed. "Thank you. You are a matchless partner, lady."

"You flatter me, sir."

"I speak only the plain truth, lady."

She pointed to another place in the city square. "The storytellers are getting ready. We can take a seat and rest. I think you'll find their tales instructive."

They walked around the fountain. Philippa waved to an empty space on a stone bench and they sat together. He reached for her hand and took it lightly. She gave it a firm squeeze and settled next to him, putting her head on his shoulder.

An older man with a white beard and very little fuzz on his head sat on the edge of the fountain's basin and motioned for quiet. When the listeners obliged, he began:

After the world was made, the Enchanters settled in this mountain valley. The land was rich, the waters flowed freely, the trees bore fruits in season, the soil yielded its grain, the flocks and herds bore their young in abundance. The Enchanters built houses and palaces of great beauty. They lived in peace.

As time passed, others moved close to the valley. The Enchanters knew nothing of them. Zara, Nevarth, and Wessalor were the Enchanters who first saw them from afar, while dredging fine stone to put on their sledges, fine stone that would be used for their fine buildings.

They decided Wessalor would remain with the sledges while Zara and Nevarth would approach the newcomers. They came by stealth, making themselves unseen among the trees and grasses. Drawing closer, they stopped at a comfortable distance, observing the party as they set up camp. They found that the newcomers resembled themselves, though slighter in build overall. Their clothing was rough but adequate, crudely made in contrast even to the Enchanters' finely made work clothes. Their words were strange, but easily understood. As they did with each other, the Enchanters could sense the measure of a person—whether peaceful, or mercurial, or contrary. Most of all, they realized that these newcomers were not Enchanters. They had no aura of magic, though they easily responded when Zara or Nevarth reached out to soothe any outburst of distress or anger, as they did in their own land to other Enchanters.

Having observed, Zara and Nevarth rejoined Wessalor. They quickly returned to their own realm. Much discussion followed. In the end, the Enchanters determined they would make their land inaccessible to them. They would be able to see it from afar, but never reach it. Thus they continued to live in peace for a good long time.

Nevarth, however, continued to ruminate on these near-dwellers. He would go and spy on them, sometimes even walk among them, seen but appearing as one of them. The near-dwellers became more numerous. They built cities. They farmed the land. They fashioned tools. They married, raised and educated children, mourned their dead. All those things the Enchanters did also.

But one thing the near-dwellers did, one thing that greatly perplexed the Enchanters: they went to war. When Nevarth returned from his journeys with reports of battles, the Enchanters were at once bewildered and alarmed. The Enchanters had disagreements and conflicts, yes. But no murders, no wars. They kept their borders guarded and remained at peace.

While the Enchanters were long-lived, they were not immortal. As centuries passed, their numbers slowly but unquestionably decreased as fewer children were born and older generations passed on. Wise as they were, the Enchanters realized the time would come when there would not be enough of them to farm their land, manage their herds, mine and refine their ores, maintain their houses and palaces.

Wessalor was first to say perhaps they should let in some of the near-dwellers, ones who were peaceable. Nevarth supported him, adding that he had found that beyond simply soothing them, as Enchanters did among their own, he could actually control them, bend them to his will, so that it did not matter which sort of near-dwellers lived among them. Zara disagreed, saying it was not their right to control others. Nevarth insisted that since they were not Enchanters, it was their right to control them.

This idea greatly distressed the other Enchanters. No one took the part of Nevarth. But Wessalor's idea still seemed good to everyone, and they began to make plans for the near-dwellers to come: how would they approach them? Once here, where would they live: apart from the Enchanters or with them? How would their needs be met?

In all this, Nevarth continue to insist that the Enchanters should simply control the near-dwellers. Alone in this thought, he became more and more estranged from the other Enchanters, until they could bear it no more. They exiled Nevarth and closed the border to him.

Years passed. Slowly, the near-dwellers came into the Enchanters' realm. At first, they lived close to each other, as the Enchanters explained their ways to the near-dwellers, and the near-dwellers explained their ways to the Enchanters. The near-dwellers seemed astonished, but pleased, that they could all understand each other's words, a simple magic among Enchanters. While their concourse was harmonious, they found their differences set them apart, and eventually they agreed to separate their communities.

The main difference was that the near-dwellers were accustomed to having a hierarchy of leaders with defined responsibilities. Zara suggested they choose their own. The near-dwellers suggested the Enchanters choose them. After much talking, both groups settled on the Enchanters choosing a monarch in this manner: any near-dweller wishing to rule would come to the Enchanter's main palace on a certain day. The Enchanters would read those gathered and determine who would be best to rule. A crown fashioned by the near-dwellers would be placed on a throne there. At midnight, the candidates would try to lift the crown from the seat. Whoever was able to lift it would be the Enchanter's choice.

Thus the first monarch was chosen. Upon death, or abdication, or when judged unable to rule by the Enchanters, there would be another gathering.

Peace reigned for many generations. Unknown to the rest of the Enchanters, Nevarth schemed to return. He lived among the peoples in the unenchanted countries, slowly learning their ways, using his magic to win them over. At last, he began gathering others to him, promising them riches if they helped him conquer these lands.

But the Enchanters became aware of him from afar, and when Nevarth came with his armies, they combined their powers and drove them off with fear, preserving their wreckage as a warning to others.

But Nevarth was not daunted. Again, he waited for generations and gathered his forces. Again, he was repelled.

And so it has been. We live in peace and security, knowing that the Enchanters will keep us in safety, even unseen.

Chapter 5

Alden and Philippa sat quietly together for a time after the storyteller finished and most of the listeners wandered elsewhere in the city square.

Eventually, Philippa looked up at Alden. "Did it answer your questions?"

"Some. Now that I have heard the story, I have other questions."

"Which questions?"

"If there's no inheritance from the rulers, why are their offspring princes and princesses?"

"It's a courtesy. The title lasts only as long as the ruler does."

"Why, then, do the young men who come in to solve the riddle of the princesses think they're going to be king?"

"Because that's what marrying a princess means in much of the rest of the world...the world they know, at least. Some here amuse themselves with these young men by going along with the foolery."

"Have any of the young men realized the truth?"

"Yes, and some leave when they realize they're not getting a crown. Others stay to solve the mystery."

"...and go when they can't solve it?"

"They seem to feel humiliated when they can't."

Alden tilted his head. "Better that they leave, then."

Philippa nodded.

"How long has it been since anyone has seen an Enchanter?" Alden asked. "I take it from listening to others that it has been a long time."

Philippa bowed her head and took a breath before meeting Alden's eye and answering. "There are some who claim to have seen them. But very few, and even those are often disbelieved. However, there is evidence of them, especially at the gleaning."

"Gleaning?"

"Yes. Whenever the flocks and crops are gathered in, some is left behind for the Enchanters. Overnight, all that has been set aside disappears."

"The price for their protection and their help?"

She inclined her head slightly. "It's an exchange we gladly partake in. They do not take too much, and we are not left with too little."

"A mutually beneficial arrangement."

"We think so."

At that point, Raven and Juno approached. Raven carried an infant and sat next to Philippa so that Raven was on one side, and Alden on the other. She handed the infant to Philippa, who smiled and cradled the baby in her arms.

Alden looked at the baby. "Beautiful child."

Raven faced him. "Our niece, Astra."

Alden turned from Raven to Philippa. Now that it had been pointed out to him, he could see the family resemblance.

"Is her mother about?" He scanned the city square to see if he could spot another woman who might remind him of Philippa.

Philippa let out a small sigh. "Foster mother."

"She's being fostered because our parents don't know about her," Raven explained.

Alden drew his head back. "How do you hide a pregnancy?"

Juno, who sat on the bench next to Raven, spoke. "It's more common than you might think. The right clothing can do wonders. You might be surprised how often we get requests to make such clothing. And, on rare occasions, larger women don't even know they're pregnant until the labor pains set in."

"I would think, from what I've been told, that it wouldn't be necessary to hide a pregnancy here," Alden said. "I was given to understand that the population was peaceful."

"There are other reasons to hide a pregnancy," Raven said. "Our parents would be dreadfully disappointed."

"As would his parents," Philippa added.

"Peaceful we are, but we have the same weaknesses as everyone else," Juno said. "I'm sure you know the familiar story: overwhelmed by attraction, she thinking she couldn't get pregnant, he thinking he wasn't able to father a child...and it all happens anyway."

"Have they married?" Alden asked.

"Secretly, of course," Raven said. "Although it was difficult to find a magistrate trustworthy enough to keep the secret."

"I would hasten to add," Juno said, "that people here don't spurn the issue of unmarried parents as we've heard happens in some unenchanted lands."

Alden nodded. "I can't imagine that they can keep this a secret forever."

Raven and Philippa exchanged a look. Raven said, "Yes, we know that eventually there will be a time when the grandparents find out. But now is not the time."

"Do they ever visit the baby?" Alden asked.

"As much as they can," Raven said.

"Do they ever see each other?" Alden asked.

"Every night." Philippa turned to Alden. "This isn't widely known, however. You know how people talk."

Alden nodded. "You can trust my discretion."

Raven gave him a wide smile. "That's the reason we told you."

"I am honored by your trust."

Juno leaned in Alden's direction. "By the way, your suit for the next royal ball is almost ready. You can come in for a fitting at any time."

Philippa looked panicked. "He's going to the ball?"

Raven turned to her. "Of course."

"He can't go," Philippa insisted.

"Why not?" Raven said.

Philippa pressed her lips together before answering. "You know why not."

At first, Alden was puzzled by this exchange. Then he said, "Oh."

The women turned to him.

Alden smiled at Philippa, put a hand over his heart, and bowed slightly from the waist. "Philippa, I promise, my heart is true."

Philippa's expression went from alarm to confusion.

"I am not a man to give in to every flirtatious glance. Though I dance with a thousand ladies, I will be thinking only of you."

Philippa's expression softened somewhat.

His hand remained over his heart. "My word is my bond."

Raven leaned close to speak into Philippa's ear. "We can rely on his discretion," she said softly. Turning to Alden, she added, "You would not betray my sister in any way."

"Not in any way."

Raven again faced Philippa, who sighed and relaxed a little.

Alden put his hand down. "I had a thought. Why don't I pay Juno and Raven to sew a gown for you, and we can go to the ball together?"

"No!" all three women said at once.

Startled by the shouting, the baby began to wail. Philippa bounced the baby slightly in her arms, and the child quieted.

At last, Alden took a breath. "Oh, I see. You don't want your customers at the coin exchange to think you're putting on airs."

Raven responded first. "There's more truth in that than you know."

The next time Alden went fishing with Jacob, he was more prepared. He brought back the basket they had used before, as well as a walking staff. Although the day had started out sunny, clouds had started to gather in the afternoon, and by the time Alden reached Jacob's shop, the sun was obscured.

Again, Jacob led the way, sure-footed, while Alden picked his way along, glad for the staff, for the light within the forest was dim. When they reached the stream, Jacob set his chain of hooks on the ground and turned to face Alden, who was not far behind.

"Need a cloak?" Jacob asked.

As Alden drew even, he could see a gray hooded cloak hanging from the high branch of a nearby tree.

Jacob gave it a tug, but it held. "Seems too large for me."

Alden leaned his staff against a thick tree and placed the basket near Jacob's chain. He walked over, reached up, and gently removed the cloak from the branch's grasp. Examining it as well as he could in the dim light, it seemed new and well-made of a thick cloth. "Yes, I think I can use this." He folded it and placed it on the ground next to the staff.

After they had caught and gathered the fish, Jacob walked ahead, holding the basket with the fish and folded chain. Alden put the cloak on and followed, holding the staff. Strangely, though the clouds had not thinned or parted, Alden found he could see ahead better than when he had walked in.

When they reached the city limits, Jacob stopped and turned. Looking directly in Alden's direction, he said tentatively, "Alden?"

"Right here."

Jacob thrust his head forward. "I can barely see you."

Alden put a hand on Jacob's forearm. "I'm here."

Jacob grasped Alden's forearm with his free hand. "There. Let's walk together."

Side-by-side, they made their way to Quentin and Matilda's. The walks were not crowded by any means, but Alden was bumped twice on the way. Each time, he got a "Sorry, I didn't see you" from the other.

After they strode through the inn's door, Jacob let go of Alden and ambled to the counter.

Quentin, standing behind the counter, faced the front door Alden had just closed behind him and squinted. "I'm going to have to light the lamps early today." He reached for a lighted taper and began to do so.

The regulars at the counter also turned in Alden's direction as he took off the cloak and draped it over an arm.

"Oh, there you are," Timicin said as Alden approached. "I didn't see you come in."

Deval nodded at the cloak. "Looks as if you found an enchanter's gift."

"Seems so," Alden said, stroking the cloth.

Khalil stepped from his seat to get a closer look. "Quality cloth, quality stitching. It's an enchanter gift, all right."

"Don't part with it, for any price," Bennu advised. "We've found that enchanter gifts go to those who can most use it."

"It fits me well," Alden said. "I was planning to keep it."

"...as if it was made especially for you," Gerasim said.

Alden smiled. "I'll put this in a safe place and join you when dinner's ready."

* * *

When Alden came in for his fitting, Juno had him change behind a screen and then stand in the middle of the room with his arms raised while she and Raven circled him, making adjustments.

"Is the codpiece comfortable?" Juno asked.

"Yes. Very. Thank you."

Raven exchanged a grin with Juno. "Shall we decorate it?"

"No," Alden said. "My father always said that a man decorating his codpiece was one who was trying to make up for a lack on the inside."

Raven lightly patted Alden's arm. "Good man."

Juno started stitching on his jacket. Alden hoped she was experienced enough not to stick him with the needle.

"So," Juno said, "how goes it with Philippa? We see the two of you in the city square almost every midday."

"Very well," Alden said. "When we are apart, I have been searching for a place where I—and then we—can live."

"I wouldn't do that just yet," Raven said, and when Alden lifted a quizzical eyebrow, added, "However, I think that you could probably steal a kiss."

"I think I shall win the lady's affection faster if kisses be given, not stolen," Alden said.

"Oh, I would say that you've already won," Raven said.

Juno turned to look Alden in the face. "You know how sisters talk." She returned to sewing.

Alden smiled. "Welcome news. I still tread carefully, however, as she appears at times skittish."

Raven nodded. "I think she fears you'll discover the family secret and lose your affection."

"Family secret?" Alden prompted.

Raven grinned again. "If I told you what it was, it wouldn't remain secret, would it?"

Alden nodded slightly, remembering what Rose said about not prying. "That's fair. Though I cannot imagine what secret she would have that would alter my feelings for her."

"Nor I. But she holds it closely, and I think there is wisdom in that. Nonetheless, I believe there would be no harm if she held it a little less closely."

"Then I shall remain while she considers when she might be ready to open her hand."

* * *

The regulars had just come in, and Alden was getting ready to go to Jacob's, when the door slammed open. Jacob stumbled in, sobbing. They crowded around him, and though he seemed to try to explain what was distressing him, they could not understand what he was saying. Alden guided him to a chair and gently pushed Jacob into it. Quentin handed him a mug of beer.

Jacob composed himself enough to take a sip. Placing the mug back on the table, he squeaked, "Rose is dead."

"What?" several voices said.

Jacob took out a handkerchief and wiped his face. "She's dead."

"When?" Alden asked.

Jacob took a long breath. "Juno came to give Rose the clothes she embroidered. She came back into the shop and told me that I needed to see to Rose. I came in and...she's dead." He began sobbing again.

Gerasim put a hand on his shoulder. "I'll go take care of Rose."

Khalil leaned in. "I'll get your apprentice and meet you there."

Gerasim nodded.

Jacob stood. "No, I don't want to stay here. I want to go home."

"I'll come with you," Alden said.

While the others expressed brief condolences, Gerasim took Jacob's left arm and Alden took his right, and together they made their way back to Jacob's shop.

The doors had been closed, and a sign had been put up: *Closed until further notice.*

"Juno must have done that," Gerasim said in a low voice.

Alden nodded.

The doors were not locked. Alden opened them and closed them again when the others had stepped through.

Inside the house, they found Juno and Raven hovering over Rose's chair. Rose had slumped into it, eyes half-closed, a threaded needle still in one hand and a handkerchief in the other.

"We didn't want to move her until you came," Juno said to Gerasim.

Gerasim nodded and turned to Jacob. "Do you want to say goodbye?"

Jacob shook his head numbly and sat in the chair nearest to Rose.

Gerasim turned to the others. "There's time."

Raven knelt by Jacob. "Jacob, can Juno and I take Rose's sewing to our shop so that her customers can get their things from us?"

Jacob nodded.

After exchanging sympathetic looks with Alden and Gerasim, Juno and Raven went through Rose's sewing stack and set aside a number of items.

Alden approached them. "Do you need help?"

Juno faced him and took a breath. "No," she said softly. "Rose tags everything she's sold or working on with her customer's names. We can find them."

"The rest we'll leave behind," Raven said. "Jacob can use them, donate them, or do whatever he wants."

Alden went back to stand next to Jacob's chair. Gerasim also waited patiently while Juno and Raven gathered the clothing, then stopped to give Jacob their condolences on the way out. Jacob acknowledged them with a nod but said nothing.

At last, there was a soft knock at the door.

"Come in," Gerasim called.

Khalil came in with a man Alden presumed was Gerasim's apprentice. They carried an open wooden coffin with a shroud tucked inside.

"Jacob?" When there was no response, Gerasim knelt beside him. "Jacob. It's time for Rose to go. We'll take good care of her."

Wordlessly, Jacob rose and stroked Rose's hair. He kissed her forehead and stepped back. Alden stood with him as the other three men gently removed Rose from the chair, wrapped her with the shroud, and placed her in the coffin. They each offered condolences to Jacob and started to file out.

"I'll stay with him, at least overnight," Alden said. "Tell Quentin."

Gerasim nodded and left.

Jacob sat in the chair again.

"I'll secure the doors and light the lamps," Alden said to Jacob.

Jacob nodded.

As he reached the doors to the shop, he heard a soft knock and opened the door slightly to see Philippa standing there, a basket in her hand.

"Jacob can't cook," she explained. "I brought dinner."

"Thank you, much obliged." He took the basket and put it on a table.

"How is Jacob doing?" she asked.

"He's not saying much. Probably still stunned."

She shook her head sadly. "Rose was all he had in the world."

"I know. I'm staying with him, overnight, at least."

"I'm glad someone he knows is staying with him."

The door pushed open a little more, and Bennu came into view. He handed Alden his rucksack. "Thought you might need this," he said. "Quentin guessed you might want to stay here for a time and opened the door to your room so we could gather some of your things. Hope you don't mind."

Alden smiled. "Not at all. Thank you."

Philippa exchanged a look with Bennu. "We'll be going."

"But if you need help, send for us," Bennu said. "Or send for Quentin."

"Thank you. I'll remember." When they were gone, Alden secured the door and took the basket into the house. Jacob remained sitting in the chair, head down.

"Dinner, Jacob," Alden said. He set the basket on am empty chair and lit the lamps. It dispelled some of the gloom. Then he found what he needed to set the table and laid out the food from the basket.

He hovered over Jacob and put an arm around his shoulders. "Come, let's have dinner. Aren't you hungry?"

Jacob put his hands on the chair's armrests and levered himself up. He went to the sink to wash up and sat in his usual chair. Alden made sure to sit in the guest chair, leaving Rose's chair at the dinner table unoccupied.

They ate in silence. When Jacob's plate was empty, he put his elbows on the table and rested his head in his hands. "What am I going to do?"

"You're going to fix things in your shop. You're going to go fishing and bring Quentin fish so Matilda can cook fish stew."

"But I'll be all alone."

"I'll be here as long as you need me."

Jacob lifted his head and looked around the room. "But you can't stay here forever."

"I'm sure the Sisters of Charity will take you in."

Jacob shook his head. "No! No, that place is for old people... old people who sit in chairs and wither away. Not for me."

Alden felt it best to restrain the impulse to remind Jacob that he was an old person. "I'm sure that Quentin and Matilda could have a room for you as long as you wanted one. I've been there for a time, and their inn always seems to have a spare room for someone who needs one."

Jacob shook his head slightly.

"Well, there's time. My grandfather always said, given enough time, a way will be found."

"Maybe so."

Alden stood. "Here, I'll wash the dishes and put away the leftovers. You can sit and rest."

When he had finished cleaning up, he spotted Jacob sitting in a chair, leaning back into the upholstery, eyes closed. Alden stepped lightly so as not to disturb him. He looked around the room and saw a pegboard on a shelf. Taking it down, he recognized it as a game that they would play in the field. A simple one: a long, narrow board with two rows of holes. Two narrow pegs to fit into the holes. Each player rolled the dice and moved the peg that number of holes forward. The first to reach the end won. Searching further, he found the dice.

When he took it down, he found Jacob watching him.

"Would you like to play?" Alden asked.

Jacob nodded and gestured at Alden to place everything on a table. Alden took a chair and they played several games.

At last, Jacob said, "I think I'll turn in." He walked over to the bed, pulled the covers, and stopped with a pained expression. Alden knew he was thinking of the empty place in the bed that Rose had occupied.

"If you can spare a blanket, I'll just sleep on the floor," Alden said to distract him.

"No need." Jacob reached under the bed and pulled out another bed, though it was not as high or as wide as Jacob's bed. "It was for our...boy." He turned around and sat on his own bed with a thoughtful expression.

"I'm sorry," Alden said. "I didn't mean...."

Jacob waved a hand and smiled. "It's all right. I have good memories of him. He would have wanted his bed to be of use to someone." He pushed the bed toward Alden. "Better than sleeping on the floor."

Alden examined the bed. It had blankets and a pillow. Not much more than a cot, but definitely better than sleeping on the floor.

Alden awoke to the sound of humming. Sitting in bed, he saw Jacob, back to him, standing at the kitchen counter. Alden got out of bed and walked over.

Jacob was slicing bread. He turned when Alden came near. "Sleep well?"

"Yes, and you?"

Jacob nodded. He motioned to a basket. "Juno left this outside the shop door this morning with a note. Our breakfast."

They sat and ate in silence. Alden felt it would be intruding on Jacob's grief to speak first, so he simply observed the older man. He seemed composed. His table manners were no different than when Rose had been at the table.

They cleaned up when they were finished. Alden used the facilities in the back, washed up, shaved. Jacob already seemed to have shaved himself.

A knock at the door, presumably the one to the shop, caught their attention.

"I'll get it." Alden went through the house door, though the shop, and opened the shop door.

Reverend Whitcomb from the Protestant church stood there, holding a book to his chest. "I hope I'm not interrupting."

"Not at all. Come in."

When they were in Jacob's living room, Whitcomb shook Jacob's hand. "I am so sorry that we lost Rose. She was beloved by many, including my wife and I. Shall we sit at the table and plan her service?"

Jacob nodded. They each took a seat at the table. Alden sat quietly as Whitcomb and Jacob made the plans. Jacob spoke calmly and clearly and showed no signs of distress.

At last, Whitcomb stood. "I'll take my leave, then." He nodded to Alden. "Alden."

"I'll show you out," Alden offered.

Jacob made no objection, no move to follow, so Alden and Whitcomb walked to the door.

When they reached it, Alden said to Whitcomb, "Jacob seems amazingly calm, considering how upset he was yesterday."

Whitcomb smiled. "Another gift from the Enchanters. I felt it myself when my sister died when I was young. Just after it happened, we were distraught. My mother was nearly inconsolable. After we went to bed, however, we were all overwhelmed by a deep sleep. In the morning, everything had changed. Not that we dismissed my sister...not at all. But it seemed that we could then remember her fondly, lovingly, and found the strength to go on. As a pastor, I see it time after time after a loss...after Rose and Jacob's loss of each of their children, for instance. It's as if the Enchanters make room for the peace that passes all understanding to penetrate our hearts and minds."

When Reverend Whitcomb walked away, Alden moved to close the shop door, but a brown-haired man rushed forward.

"I know that Rose just died, and I'm so sorry, but I really need my table and Jacob said it would be fixed today." He held out a hand. "I have the money. Can you just give me the table?"

As Alden drew a breath to respond, he felt a gentle tap on his shoulder. He turned to see Jacob behind him.

"Let's open the shop," he said softly.

"Are you sure?" Alden said.

Jacob nodded.

They pushed the large wooden doors wide open. The brown-haired man followed Jacob as he walked to the back of the shop, expressing condolences and apologizing.

Jacob said nothing but nodded and handed over a small table. The man counted out coins in Jacob's hand, again expressed his condolences, and left quickly.

Jacob deposited the coins through a slot in a box resting on a bench. He turned and proceeded to the front of the shop, and when Alden turned to follow him, he saw a group of people standing silently, expectantly. When Jacob reached them, some expressed condolences, others handed him baskets of food, and some apologetically asked Jacob to repair something. ("I'm sorry to disturb you. I'm so sorry to hear about Rose, we all loved her, but I really need this fixed right away...could you?")

Jacob handed the food baskets to Alden, who put them in the house. When he returned, there were more to put in the house. On his way in and out, Alden saw Jacob taking things to be fixed.

Close to midday, however, there came a respite.

Jacob turned to the accumulation of items to be fixed and turned to Alden. "Do you know how to put broken things back together?"

"I've done some simple repairs out in the field. Nothing fancy."

Jacob nodded. "I don't do much fancy work. If people want fancy, they take their things down the street. If they bring them to me, it means they want it fast, and aren't fussy about how, as long as it works again."

"Then, if you can show me where you keep your hammers and nails, I'll do what I can."

They set to work. Alden thought, as he started to make repairs, that keeping hands and mind occupied was probably good for Jacob at this point. Sometimes they worked separately, other times Jacob came over and showed him how to do carpentry work and supervised Alden's repairs.

When the midday bell rang, Jacob dusted off his hands and turned to Alden. "Let's close up the shop. I want to go see Rose."

Once the doors were secure, Jacob led the way to Gerasim's. On the way, a few people stopped to shake Jacob's hand and extend brief condolences.

When they reached the funeral parlor, Gerasim greeted them and led them inside. "Rose is in the back. I'd like you to look at some of our finer caskets and see which ones you want."

Jacob bowed his head briefly. "I can't afford much."

Gerasim smiled. "Seems that Quentin and Matilda took up a collection last night when word got around. Whatever casket you want is paid for, and they paid Khalil to carve a headstone, too."

Jacob lifted his head with a faint smile, the first smile Alden had seen on Jacob since Rose had died.

Alden and Gerasim stood back as Jacob sat with Rose's body, still in the wooden coffin, for a time. Rose was only uncovered from the waist up, but she had been washed, her hair had been combed, and her clothes had been arranged neatly.

After Jacob had paid his respects and selected a casket, they walked outside. Jacob said he was hungry, so Alden paid street vendors for sausages and cider for them both. The vendors offered their goods for free, considering Jacob's situation, but Alden paid them anyway.

Khalil's stonemason shop was nearby. He welcomed both men and talked to Jacob about the size and shape of the headstone, as well as which carvings he wanted. Besides Rose's name, they settled on a carving of a rosebud.

When that was done, they went back to the shop. As Jacob unlocked the doors, he turned to Alden. "I'd like to take a nap."

Alden nodded. "Is it all right with you if I stay in the shop and keep working?"

Jacob nodded.

Alden spent the afternoon doing whatever repairs he could, setting things aside if they proved too complicated for him. People came in wanting their things. They were able to point them out and seemed to know how much to pay. Alden collected the money, handed over the items, and dropped the coins in the box. Others simply came to offer condolences or drop off more baskets of food, which Alden set quietly inside the house so as not to disturb Jacob.

Toward late afternoon, Jacob came out of the house with his fishhooks.

"You're sure you want to go fishing?" Alden asked.

Jacob nodded.

They closed up the shop and went fishing as usual. Quentin and Matilda's inn was empty as they entered.

"The others are working late," Quentin explained. "Gerasim and Khalil are busy with their work, Bennu is arranging flowers for the funeral, Timicin is getting pots to put them in, and Deval is working with his guard unit to plan how to get people in and out of the church in an orderly manner."

Alden took advantage of the time to talk to Jacob and Quentin about moving in with Jacob for the time being, packing what was left in his room and getting the bundles ready to go.

"Matilda and I will miss you," Quentin said. "I suppose you won't be working in the kitchen?"

"I hope it won't be too much of an inconvenience?"

"No, we managed before you came here and we'll manage again, but we will miss you, that's a fact."

Alden smiled. "I'm sure you'll continue to see me at dinnertime."

"I'm counting on it."

The next morning after breakfast, Jacob and Alden rummaged though Rose's stack of ready-made clothes to find a funeral outfit for Alden and managed to put together something decent. Jacob told Alden to keep the outfit.

The church, which was normally half-empty on a Sunday, was filled for the service. Jacob and Alden were escorted to a reserved area in the front. Late comers stood at the side, or in the aisles, or in the choir loft (which had a choir, though they did not fill the entire space). The service was fitting. Reverend Whitcomb gave a eulogy about Rose and what she meant to the community. Jacob stood in front and said a few words before returning to his seat. At the end of the service, Deval and his guardsmen took the casket outside to the nearby cemetery, where Reverend Whitcomb said a few more words at the graveside and dismissed the crowd. Jacob lingered while the casket was lowered, then took a rose from the floral display that had been on top of the casket and tossed it in. Alden followed suit and followed as Jacob walked silently back to the shop. The shop remained closed. Jacob and Alden passed the afternoon with the dice and peg game, then went fishing in the late afternoon.

Chapter 6

In the days that followed, Alden quickly learned the ins and outs of basic carpentry. With an assistant to help Jacob, the repairs became more "fancy" and less crude.

One day, Juno came to the shop with Alden's finished outfit. Handing over the bundle, she added, "Tomorrow night. Are you getting excited?"

Alden shrugged. "More curious than excited, I suppose."

"You'll have plenty to keep you occupied, what with the dances and the food and the gossip."

"I take it you've been to one."

"One or two," Juno said coyly.

"Are you going to this one?"

"If you see me, you'll know," she said with a sly smile, and ambled away.

Jacob came to the front of the shop. "Folks sure do get wound up about these things."

Alden turned to him. "Have you ever been to a ball?"

He shook his head. "Not one for dancing, myself. Rose went to a ball before we started courting, mostly to see the fancy clothes. She said one was enough."

Juno and Raven had briefed Alden about the royal balls during the fittings, so he knew when to go and what to do, at least enough to get in. People started to line the streets in the late afternoon to watch those who walked to the castle in their finery. The streets were largely empty by the time Alden joined the throng. Looking around as he sauntered down the road, he saw others, mostly couples, dressed as spectacularly as he was, chatting among themselves as they strode ahead and behind him. Those on the walkways would pause and point and talk to those next to them.

When Alden was about a stone's throw from the castle gates, he stopped and stood to one side. Here the walkways had been cleared by the guards. Alden quickly scanned the men in uniform to see whether Deval was among them, but apparently his unit was not on duty that evening.

There was no moat, but there was a drawbridge across a chasm. The castle, as had been reported to him, had been built along the side of a mountain, which was more-or-less the castle's northwest wall. The white stone was polished and glowed in the late afternoon sun. Lights shone through the many windows.

"I never get tired of admiring it myself," said a voice next to him.

Alden turned and saw an elegantly-dressed man, who seemed to be about this age. He looked vaguely familiar, but Alden could not quite place him.

The man extended an arm and pointed. "As you can see, the ground making the foundation rises from there and meets the mountain and the forest in the back."

"Are you a builder, sir?" Alden asked.

"No," the man said pleasantly. "But I can appreciate a good design." He turned to face Alden squarely. "There is an enchantment within."

Alden turned to the castle and then back to the man. "That would not be surprising, considering who built the castle and the mysteries of the princesses."

"More surprising than you would know." He held out a hand. Alden could see a ring in his palm, a beautiful silver band with no stone. "Here, take this. It will give you eyes to see what others may not."

"A gift?" Alden said cautiously.

"There are gifts all around. Those who are wise will accept what they need." When Alden did not respond right away, he added, "Will you give me your hand?"

Alden extended an arm. The man placed the ring on one of his fingers. "Guard it well. It is not for others."

Before Alden could answer, a bell in a castle tower sounded. Alden looked up. When he looked down again, the man was gone. Alden turned an entire circle, but the man was nowhere to be seen.

"Missing someone?"

Alden turned again and saw Deval standing within reach. A woman in elegant clothes stood at his side.

"I was talking to someone," Alden explained, "and then, he disappeared."

Deval gestured ahead. "Probably answering the bell. It's the signal for everyone to get inside." He turned to the woman holding on to his arm. "My wife, Priya."

Alden bowed politely. "An honor to make your acquaintance, lady."

Priya nodded. "An honor to meet you, sir. I have heard so much about you."

"All good news!" Deval affirmed. "Shall we go in before they shut the doors?"

Alden followed them as they led the way across the drawbridge, then through a wide, long hallway, and then to an enormous room with a high ceiling. Between the light coming through the stained glass windows, the chandeliers, the candelabras, and the reflections from many mirrors along the walls, Alden could see everything and everyone clearly. On one side, carpeted stairs led to two ornate thrones, currently empty. Near the wall opposite the throne, tables had been set up with delectable food and drink. Chairs had been set up near another wall, some occupied, some not. Many guests stood in this area. And along the wall opposite the chairs were musicians tuning instruments. The main part of the room was empty. The tiles on floor had been set in decorative designs.

"Impressive, isn't it?" Deval said.

"Yes," Alden said, taking it all in.

"My great-uncle was king before King Reginald," Deval said. "I spent many hours here as a child. We were allowed to explore. I know the castle very well."

Priya leaned over. "And I have a great-great-great grandmother who was a reigning queen."

Deval touched Alden's shoulder. "Let's move to a better viewing spot. I'll point out the princesses."

"Oh. Thank you," Alden said.

"If you gentlemen will excuse me," Priya said, "I see a friend over there."

Alden nodded at her. "Pleasure meeting you, lady."

She nodded and smiled. "Pleasure meeting you, Alden."

Deval ushered Alden to a place near the thrones, but a respectful distance away. Along the way, Alden saw that there was a crowd, though the largeness of the room might cause one to underestimate the numbers.

Deval touched Alden's shoulder and gestured. "That's Princess Electra, the eldest. Very learned, they say, but hard to get to know."

Alden looked in the direction Deval indicated. Electra's face was powdered and she wore a large powdered wig. Each cheek had a large red dot painted on it.

"Next to Electra," Deval continued, "is Ilona, the next eldest. Then there's Lydia, next to her. Rhea, fourth in line, is known for spending the most time on the dance floor. You can probably get a dance with her."

"How does one approach a princess to ask?" Alden said.

Deval smiled. "One doesn't. Either the king will invite you to dance with one of his daughters, or, if you can get close to a princess, you can state politely that it would be an honor to have this dance, at which point the princess will ask if she is interested."

"I appreciate the instruction."

"That doesn't apply to the women who aren't royals. You can ask at will...or they can ask you."

"Can one politely decline?"

"One can. There is no lack of partners here, as you can see. There are also men-only and women-only dances. Those are announced by a herald in advance." Deval extended an arm again. "The one Rhea is talking to is Thalia, who's next in line to her. Then there's Olympia and Vinia, followed by Brigitta, and then the triplets."

"Triplets," Alden repeated, impressed.

"Yes. Arabella, Alinora, and Alesia." Deval lowered his voice. "It's said that they make brandy in the lower levels of the castle."

Alden raised an eyebrow.

Deval smiled conspiratorially. "No one has ever caught them at it, though."

"I'll keep their secret."

Deval gestured again. "The last one is Lark. She's the youngest and smallest of the princesses. Given to melancholy, they say."

"Any reason?"

Deval shook his head. "None that I know of. Temperament, perhaps."

Alden took a second look at all the princesses. Only Electra had a powdered face. The others all wore elegant masks— embroidered, sequined, or jeweled masks. None of them wore a crown or tiara, though some had jewels or beads woven into their hair. Some wore necklaces or bracelets or rings. Some had no other adornment.

Horns sounded from the other side of the room.

"Their majesties, King Reginald and Queen Beatrice," a herald announced.

Curtains at the end of the room parted and the royal couple entered in full regalia. Alden admired the work in the crowns and the cloaks. They each walked in front of their respective thrones and faced the crowd.

"Welcome, friends," Reginald said. "Please partake of our hospitality. You may choose your partners for the first dance."

People started to move.

Alden turned to Deval. "Finding Priya?"

Deval laughed companionably. "It's commonplace here to dance with someone other than your spouse or sweetheart. It's presumed that one can dance with them at anytime, though it's not forbidden, either, and some couples dance exclusively with their lovers." He nodded. "I think I see a cousin over there who expects me."

When Deval walked away, a woman approached Alden, looked him in the eye, and curtsied. "May I have this dance, sir?"

Alden bowed and held out an arm. "I would be honored, lady."

The music started and Alden recognized it as a minuet. He went through the figures with the woman. She was obviously practiced, but not as expert as Philippa.

When the music stopped, Alden's partner curtsied and joined a number of dancers heading toward the food tables. Alden looked around for Deval and spotted a man in royal livery walking toward him.

"The king requests your presence," he said, and turned to lead the way.

Alden walked up the stairs. Reaching the top, he stopped and bowed low. "Your majesties." Straightening again, he found Queen Beatrice in his direct line of sight. Seeing her face this closely, he froze.

"Your expression speaks consternation, friend," Reginald queried.

Alden took a breath and faced the king squarely. "Truly, Your Majesty, I have seen queens from one end of the continent to the next, and none have matched the beauty of Her Majesty. It takes one's breath away."

Beatrice smiled. "You are fair spoken, sir."

"Alden, Your Majesty, at your service." He bowed again.

"You have been much spoken about, Alden," Reginald said. "With some reputation as a dancer."

"I have some small experience, Your Majesty."

"More than that, or so I have been given to understand." Reginald turned and extended his hand in Electra's direction. She stepped forward and took it. Reginald faced Alden and said, "I would be pleased if you would dance with my daughter."

Alden bowed to Electra. "My honor and pleasure, Your Royal Highness."

Electra showed no emotion whatsoever as Alden took her hand. It was all he could do to keep his hand from trembling... and was hers trembling, too, even ever so slightly? But she did not face Alden as he escorted her down the stairs.

Alden, however, could not help but look at Electra. As soon as he saw her mother, he knew. But he had to be true to his word, not to betray her. There was no doubt, of course, that she knew who he was. Every moment they had together simply confirmed who she was. He knew the curve of her neck, the lift of her chin, the shape of her nose, and especially, the touch of her hand. No amount of powder could disguise those.

When they reached the dance floor, they faced each other.

"Your Royal Highness, it is not my aim to inconvenience you in any way. You need not speak, and I am not here to press you into speaking. But, since we are commanded to dance together, shall we just...dance...and take what pleasure there is in the harmony of the steps?"

Her expression softened a little. The music started, they drew together as partners in movement, and after that, he was dancing with the Philippa he knew.

When the music stopped, Alden escorted Electra up the stairs. At the top, Reginald waited, holding Princess Rhea's hand. Rhea wore a wide, knowing smile.

"My daughter Rhea wishes to have this dance."

Alden released Electra, who moved away quickly and smoothly. He bowed to Rhea. "My honor and pleasure, Your Highness."

He took Rhea's hand. They descended the stairs.

Alden knew from his first dance that the music was loud enough to be heard throughout the hall, but soft enough so that partners could converse. When the music started, he found that Rhea seemed eager to do just that.

"You seem to have captured the attention of my sister."

"Did I?" Alden said innocently.

"I heartily approve."

"I am honored to have the approval of Your Highness and Her Royal Highness."

"Not only she, but my father and mother are quite impressed with you."

"Again, I am honored. In turn, I am impressed with them."

Rhea's smile never faded. "You seem to be a man with eyes to see."

Alden missed a step, but quickly corrected himself.

"I'm sorry," Rhea said. "I seem to have spoken out of turn."

"Not at all, Your Highness," Alden said. "It was my own clumsiness."

She smiled wryly. "I cannot imagine you being clumsy at anything."

"I am a man of clay, just like anyone else."

"I do not think you realize your true worth, sir. You are exceptional in many ways."

"I am but a humble servant, ma'am, and that's no false modesty speaking."

"Perhaps. Do not mistake me. We have many men of honor in this realm, and I do not devalue their worth. But I believe each of us is born with a special talent, and I think yours is to touch others' hearts with a singular clarity."

"I am honored by your compliment, Your Highness."

The music stopped.

"Please enjoy the rest of your evening," Rhea said, as they bowed to each other.

Alden took Rhea's hand to escort her back up the stairs. "I intend to."

When they reached the top of the stairs, Alden could see neither Reginald nor Beatrice.

"My parents are probably on the floor, speaking to guests," Rhea said.

"Then allow me to escort you to your seat."

Rhea nodded with a smile. Alden walked her to a place near the wall, bowed, and backed away until he could comfortably turn and proceed elsewhere.

The music played for the next dance, and most guests were on the floor. Alden strolled to a food table. As might be expected at a royal repast, he saw a wide assortment of delicacies: baked goods, confections, and fruits had been displayed in abundance. He accepted a goblet of wine from a page and began to sample, sauntering past the serving tables.

His mind on the food, he almost collided with another man and stepped back. "Your pardon."

Reginald smiled amicably. "There was no trespass. I was seeking you out."

Although his hands were full, Alden still managed a suitable bow. "Your servant, sir."

"I noticed a misstep when you were dancing with Rhea."

"Accidental, Your Majesty, I assure you. Even the most practiced dancers miss a step now and then."

"To be sure. I also noticed that you and Electra seemed to take great pleasure in the dance. Did I sense an attraction?"

Alden cleared his throat. He had anticipated someone might have noted this and was ready with an answer. "Merely my delight in having a partner with an outstanding ability in the dance. With great respect to Her Royal Highness's beauty and temperament, there is already a lady who rules my heart."

Reginald nodded. "Well, one cannot blame a father for an attempt at matchmaking. None of my girls has a sweetheart."

As far as you know, Alden thought. "There are some who choose not to marry."

"Yes, but all twelve? Ilona and Lydia have said more than once that they believe that any decent woman and any decent man can make a good match. That's the reason I felt comfortable promising a daughter's hand in marriage to anyone who can tell me how my daughters wear out a pair of shoes every night. The Enchanters would not let in any of the ruffians that I encountered in my younger days when I went with the merchants outside this realm to trade."

"How long has this been happening?"

"Several years now." He looked up briefly, as if reckoning. "Maybe more than that. Ever since the older girls came of marriageable age."

"If I may be so bold...."

"Please do."

"Perhaps it is time to put the matter to rest. Some mysteries resolve themselves, with time."

He sighed. "I'm afraid the matter has taken on a life of its own. It started when I told the girls that they would start to have chaperones if they were going outside these walls. I did not think that would be seen as unusual...even on the outside, I understand that there are rules laid down for young people so that they don't exceed their maturity."

"There is indeed. I and my brothers and sisters had supervision ourselves. But even so, I was the adventurous sort in my younger days, and escaped the notice of my elders several times...though I was held accountable afterwards."

"Yes, and it wasn't as if I wasn't expecting that. What I didn't expect was a full-on rebellion. Something is going on, and with no explanation. If it's innocent, why not explain? If it's not innocent, why not tell us so that we can help?"

"I wouldn't know."

Reginald regarded Alden soberly. "Even if your heart is taken, and I would not ask you to take it back, would you be interested in helping me resolve this? I can reward you richly." Noting Alden's hesitant expression, he added, "Please speak plainly."

Alden took a breath. "I don't know whether solving this mystery at this juncture is wise...or even possible...."

Reginald turned his head briefly. "I've been drawing near to the same conclusion. But I am not yet ready to give up."

"I wish you the best in your efforts, Your Majesty."

He placed a hand on Alden's shoulder. "I appreciate your counsel, nonetheless."

"For what it was worth, I'm pleased to have given it."

At that point, Rhea walked up. "Father, you promised me a dance, and I have come to claim it."

Reginald nodded to Alden and turned his attention to Rhea.

Alden turned around to survey the rest of the food table and found himself facing Beatrice. He bowed.

She nodded toward Rhea. "Headstrong, every one of them."

"I have not been around Their Highnesses long enough to tell one way or the other."

She smiled knowingly. "Well, I have. You've probably heard that they join us for breakfast every morning, and then disappear until the evening meal, in addition to whatever escapade they're at during the night."

"I had heard hints of it, Your Majesty."

"Word is that the triplets brew brandy in some region of the castle we don't know about...which wouldn't surprise me, since the palace always seems to have hidden parts that we didn't know about, despite generations of oral tradition passed down from one reign to the next. One of my fondest wishes is to speak to an actual Enchanter and find out where all the nooks and crannies are."

"Has anyone thought of writing things down?"

"Oh, the scribes keep a careful history. Reginald and I have poured over the volumes trying to find where the girls might have gone, without result."

"You must be comforted, however, that every morning they arrive at the breakfast table safe and whole."

She nodded. "That is very true, sir, and not unimportant. Still, from time to time, there are appearances I find troubling. Last year, for instance, I suspected that Lark might be pregnant, but it turned out to be a false pregnancy."

It was all Alden could do to keep the expression on his face from changing.

"We love our girls, and of course we know that the older ones are fully into their womanhood and may live their lives as they please within the law. But something about this whole affair is disturbing...not that I suspect the girls of malfeasance, but I do wonder whether they have become involved in a tangle that does not benefit them and that they don't know how to get out of. I just wish they would confide in us so that we could help."

"I understand your concern, Your Majesty."

"I overheard you telling Reginald that perhaps the problem was either unsolvable or would be resolved naturally in time. I sincerely hope it is the latter."

"As do I."

Beatrice took a breath. "Well, I am an elder keeping you from your dancing. Please continue."

Alden bowed. "Thank you, Your Majesty. Your hospitality is indeed excellent." He backed away a comfortable distance before turning and continuing down the table. Once at a place where there were few others around, he resumed nibbling. He had been too self-conscious to eat when talking to the monarchs.

The herald announced a woman-only dance. Alden kept eating while watching the dancers. It was not long before he spotted Rhea dancing with a partner he did not immediately recognize. Soon, however, he realized that Rhea's partner was Juno. He had a feeling while dancing with Rhea that she was Raven, and this simply confirmed that feeling.

"Are you enjoying the festivities?"

Alden turned to see Deval standing next to him, holding a goblet. "Yes, I am."

Deval nodded toward the dancers. "Priya is getting a lot of compliments on her dress."

"Yes, it's a stunning dress."

"Juno and Raven. They sewed my outfit, too."

Alden looked it over again. "Yes, I noticed it. They did well with mine, I think."

Deval nodded, sipped his drink, and turned toward the dance floor again. "They should come some time. I think they would enjoy it."

Alden lifted an eyebrow. "You've never seen them here?"

Deval shook his head. "I suggested it to Juno once. She gave an evasive answer."

"Well, perhaps one day."

Deval took another sip. "I saw you talking with the king and queen earlier."

"Yes, the queen said something to me that made me think of you."

"Oh?" Deval asked, curious.

"You said that you were free to explore the castle as a child. Her Majesty said that the castle was full of surprises. Did you ever notice any?"

"Oh, yes. The archivists here warn the incoming royalty about the mysterious happenings here. I and my brothers, sisters, and cousins were told we could explore, but not to go wandering alone. One time, my four-year-old brother wandered off by himself and disappeared for an afternoon. There was a frantic search. The cooks, the gardeners, everyone looked everywhere. After a few hours, my mother opened a door to a room she had checked before just in case she missed something, and my brother walked out. When asked where he had been, he just said 'rooms.' How did he get into the rooms? 'A door,' he said. Could he show us the door? He walked down the hall and indicated a wall, but there was no door there. A few years ago, at a family gathering, I asked him if he remembered that afternoon, and he said that what he remembered is that he opened a door and went into a room, then opened another door and went into another room, and so forth until our mother opened a door. I asked about the rooms, and he said they were regular rooms with carpeting, couches, chairs, tables, and so forth. I asked if they were dusty and he said no, everything was clean. He said he tried to find the first door again when he was older and wasn't able to."

"I take it people get lost here?"

"Frequently. You think you know where you're going and lose your way. But almost all the time, if you keep going, you'll find a place you recognize and can go from there." He took another sip. "Made the place interesting. We, that is, the children in our family, loved it. The elders in the family were more cautious."

The music ended and the herald announced a men-only dance.

Alden turned to Deval. "Going?"

"I think I'll sit this one out. You go ahead."

Alden did. This was a familiar line dance, where two groups of men arranged themselves facing each other. One group would perform steps to the music and the other group would attempt not only to imitate the steps but improve on them. From the sound of the cheering from the onlookers, Alden was certain that his group had won the most approval from the crowd.

When the dance was over, he found himself near the wall where the princesses were assembled. He noted Lark sitting at the perimeter, with what he presumed were ladies-in-waiting standing nearby.

Cautiously, Alden approached the chair where Lark sat and bowed deeply. "May I have your permission to speak a word, Your Highness?"

She nodded. "You may."

"I, too, am a younger offspring of a great house. I remember seeing my older brothers and sisters achieving success, and feeling hopeless because, compared to them, I had done nothing. In fact, I had made mistakes that I cringe to think about now. But I continued to put one foot in front of the other and make whatever small progress that I could. Gradually, I was able to build a life for myself, and take the steps I needed that eventually brought me here, where I have at last been able to find a good place for myself. If I may be so bold, I wish to say that if you find yourself in a similar place, do not lose hope. The years ahead may bring you greater happiness than you can foresee at this time."

She nodded again.

"I would be honored to have a dance with a woman who has been through so much and yet can hold her own."

She stood and extended a hand. "I would dance with you, sir, if it be your will."

He bowed. "I am your most humble and obedient servant, Your Highness." Taking her hand, he led her to the dance floor.

Lark proved to be an accomplished dancer, almost as good as her elder sister. But then, Alden thought, she did have practice every night.

When the music stopped, he escorted her back to the chair, bowed, and returned to the food tables.

Many confectionaries and several dances later, a bell sounded. Everyone turned to the thrones. Reginald and Beatrice stood together. Beatrice said, "We thank you for your presence, friends, and hope this has been an enjoyable evening for you. We take our leave now and wish you a pleasant evening." They walked off the same way they came.

Deval and Priya walked over to Alden. "The balls last until midnight, when everyone retires to their favorite gathering place and tells those who didn't come about the entire evening. Join us at Quentin and Matilda's?"

"Please give my regards and my regrets to Quentin and Matilda. I think I will take a walk and think about what I have seen."

Deval nodded. "That does tend to happen after the first ball."

Alden walked out of the castle with Deval and Priya. They separated once they reached the streets with fond farewells.

Taking a route parallel to the castle walls, Alden headed toward the forested area near the mountains at the back of the castle. The moon was full, and the castle gave off its own soft glow, so he could see well enough. For some reason, he wanted to feel close to Philippa for a while longer, and this seemed to be the best way.

He found a spot at the edge of the forest where he could see the castle clearly yet remain concealed. His experience with scouting missions served him well in finding an appropriate spot. Alden had a fleeting thought of sitting against a tree but realized that it could stain or tear his new clothes, and he wanted to keep those in prime condition. As a guard, he was accustomed to standing hours at a time; he felt that he could simply stand there and watch the castle comfortably for as long as he needed to.

The lights behind the windows in the castle went on and off as, he presumed, the castle staff wandered to and fro cleaning and organizing after the ball. Other lights, he presumed, were the castle residents moving through the halls until they reached their rooms. He wondered which ones were Philippa's.

He had stood for some time, lost in thought, when a soft glow to his left caught his attention. A tall man with a lantern came into view. He walked to the castle wall. Although he was too far away for Alden to make out features, he felt certain that this was the same man who had given him the ring, which he had not even thought about since the man had put it on his finger. He felt for it, realizing it was still there.

When the man reached the wall, Alden saw an opening appear where there had been no door only a moment ago. Holding the lantern in one hand, he reached inside the opening with the other, and drew out a woman. Again, although Alden could not see the face clearly, the form was distinctive enough for him to realize that this was Philippa. There was no powdered wig now, nor powder on her face, and her clothes...the dress was beautiful beyond anything any dressmaker could fashion, glittering and glowing with a sheen that appeared to be gold, then silver, then sapphire.

Philippa took a few steps away from the man, stopped, and turned. The man reached inside again and drew out another princess, similarly garbed. When all twelve had assembled, the opening disappeared. The man walked to the front of the line and led the princesses away.

Alden remained where he was. He debated briefly with himself as to whether he should follow and decided that now was not the time. Nor was it the time to inspect the wall, a move that was even more tempting. Instead, he walked slowly through almost deserted streets to Jacob's house, where he let himself in. Jacob had already gone to bed. Alden undressed as quietly as he could in the moonlight streaming through the windows, put on a nightshirt, and climbed into his cot.

He had settled in, and nearly gone to sleep, when he sat up with a realization. The man who had given him the ring, and who had led the princesses away from the castle, was exactly the same man he had seen in his dream in his room at Quentin and Matilda's on the first morning he had arrived.

Chapter 7

In exchange for Jacob teaching him carpentry, Alden started teaching Jacob how to cook. Jacob already knew how to light a cooking fire and keep it steady. He already knew basics such as how to bone a fish and peel vegetables. Beyond that, though, Jacob said his cooking was so bad that Rose had insisted that he leave meal preparation to her.

Jacob did seem to be eager to learn, nonetheless. Alden found that Jacob needed detailed instructions to get even simple meals edible, but once Jacob caught on, the results were more than palatable.

The morning after the ball, Alden was looking on as Jacob stirred sliced vegetables and sausage in a pan. A knock on the outside door drew their attention.

"I'll get it," Alden said.

Jacob nodded and continued to stir.

Philippa was at the door. Her face wore a worried expression. "Can we go somewhere and talk?"

Alden gestured. "The back of the shop is almost always deserted." He led the way, and, as usual, no one was there.

Philippa turned to him. "You haven't said anything to anyone about last night, have you?"

Alden took both of her hands in his and looked into her eyes. "My word is my bond. I have done and will do nothing to betray you."

She sighed. "I had thought the enchantment would have hidden us from you. But I knew when you looked at me that you had eyes to see, though I don't know how."

He smiled. "Does it matter?"

Her face was grim. "Yes, it does. If you can see through the enchantment, others can, too."

"No. I saw because I was given a gift."

"Who...?" Her expression changed. "Never mind. I know who."

"I know who, but I don't know why."

She looked at him soberly. "There is so much that I could tell you. But I, too, have given my word, and my word must be my bond."

He lifted an eyebrow. "I would guess that here, such a bond is stronger here than it might be elsewhere."

"That is the truth." She leaned forward and put her head on his chest, which required her to bend at the knees a little since she was slightly taller than he was.

He folded his arms around her.

After a few seconds of silence, she said, "You missed a step."

"My dancing partner told me that I had eyes to see. That startled me."

She pulled back slightly, and he released her. "You had a bold dancing partner," she said with a smile.

He smiled back. "I cannot but agree."

She reached out, took his hand, and looked him in the eyes. "I love you, Alden."

"And I you, Philippa."

"I trust you."

"And I you, Philippa. If you need anything of me, you need only ask. I remain your most humble and obedient servant." He bowed slightly.

"Thank you. Right now, I need to get to the shop before the brothers miss me."

"And I need to get inside before Jacob burns our breakfast."

When Alden came back into the house, Jacob said, "Was that Philippa?"

Alden nodded. "Yes."

"What did she want?"

"To talk about us, as courting couples do." Alden looked over the contents of the pan. "It's ready." He brought over the plates. Jacob spooned the contents into them. They took their breakfast and sat.

As they ate, Jacob said, "You and Philippa can live here if you want, after you wed."

Alden smiled. "I think that might be a little crowded, and I don't think that this is what Philippa has in mind for a home, nice as it is."

Jacob's face fell. "I'll be all alone."

Alden looked directly at Jacob. "Jacob, when the time comes, I give you my promise that we won't leave you all alone."

"I'm not living with the Sisters of Charity."

"Jacob, I'm not planning to leave you with the Sisters of Charity, though I'm sure living at their enclosure is not as bad as you think. You can take on a partner or an apprentice."

"You're my partner and apprentice."

"For now. Or, since you're a carpenter, you can section off part of the house and take on a boarder. I've seen many kinds of living arrangements in my travels. When the time comes, we'll find something you like."

Jacob looked thoughtful.

Before Jacob could continue the topic, Alden added, "Nothing's going to happen today. Or next week. Or probably, next month. It's something we need not think about until the time comes. Who knows? Something neither you or I could foresee could happen that we'd all be satisfied with."

As had been his habit for some time, Alden left Jacob's shop just before the midday bell and walked to the coin exchange, arriving just as Philippa closed the shop for the hour. He felt a little anxious approaching her, after the night before and the morning's conversation, but when she turned from the door and smiled at him, he knew that his fears were groundless.

They spent the hour as they usually did: buying lunch from the vendors, sitting next to each other in the city square to eat, then strolling through the streets. Their favorite spot to linger was one of the city gardens. Occasionally they saw Bennu tending the flowers and trees, though he was not there that day.

There was much of importance that Alden wanted to talk to her about, but this day seemed to be a day to relax in everyday blessings. She talked about a group of children who had come before school to exchange the slivers they had been paid for the leaves they had gathered, excited about the toys they could now buy. Alden talked about the bed he was constructing with

Jacob's guidance, to replace the cot he had been sleeping in. He had had a twinge when he first discussed this with Philippa, but she showed no awkwardness when he explained his relief that he soon would, at last, be sleeping in real bed for the first time since he had left Quentin and Matilda's.

As the hour drew to a close, he escorted her back to the coin exchange, and returned to the shop, where Jacob could still make a suitable feast for himself at midday from the food that friends and neighbors still occasionally brought to share.

That evening, when he and Jacob brought in the catch, Alden saw a new man among the four regulars at Quentin and Matilda's. He was tall and slender, with short black hair.

Jacob handed over the fish to Quentin.

Timicin turned the man so that he faced Jacob and Alden. "Jacob and Alden, this is Richard, the next king of the realm." He winked at Alden.

Jacob groaned and shook his head. "Not another one." He walked to a table and took a seat.

"Another one?" Richard said. His back had been to Timicin and could not have seen the wink.

Alden did his best not to show the deep shock he felt. Was this man going to endanger Philippa and her sisters? He needed to find out more. Extending a hand, he said, "Pleased to meet you, Richard. Are you newly arrived?"

Richard shook Alden's hand and released it. "Yes, just came in a few hours ago. Took me forever to get here."

"That's a familiar story," Khalil said.

Richard turned in Jacob's direction. "What does that mean, 'another one?'"

"It means you're not the first one to come here to try to solve the riddle of the princesses," Bennu said.

"But no one has yet succeeded?" Richard asked.

"Yes, no one has yet succeeded," Gerasim said.

Timicin guided Richard to an empty table and pushed him into the chair. The regulars also took chairs and gathered around. Leaving Jacob to sit by himself, Alden grabbed a chair and joined them.

Timicin turned to Alden. "We were just about to explain to Richard the rules of the game."

"Yes, I would like to know." Richard said.

"First," Timicin said, "you need to present yourself as a petitioner to the king and queen at their morning audience."

Alden's eyebrows went up. "There's a morning audience?"

Deval turned to him. "Yes, every day except Fridays, Saturdays, and Sundays. There's an audience room where the king and queen sit. Petitioners first go to a clerk near the door and state their requests. Minor requests are referred to a magistrate in residence in a separate room. If the clerk feels the king and queen need to hear the request, they are escorted to the audience room."

"If you say you're there to solve the riddle of the princesses," Bennu said, "you'll be escorted to the audience room."

"You'll get some instruction there," Deval said, "but we feel we can give you some additional sage advice."

"Please do," Richard said.

"First," Deval said, "do not lay traps. If you do anything that even appears might injure a princess, the castle guards will escort you directly to the border. You will not be able to re-enter."

"He knows what he's talking about," Khalil said. "His unit has been on duty when this has been attempted and he'll be the first to give you the boot."

"Wouldn't have even entered my mind," Richard said.

Alden privately doubted that but was glad that Richard had been warned.

"The crown also frowns upon destruction of property," Deval said, "such as trying to carve a door in the castle."

Richard nodded. "I'll make sure I won't."

Bennu glanced at Alden, then turned back to Richard. "You'll also want to avoid the enchanted forest."

"Why?"

"People come to grief there," Bennu said.

"Oh, that's nonsense," Jacob called from his seat. "Alden and I go there all the time."

"Alden and Jacob are the only ones we know who can enter and come back safely," Gerasim said.

Richard turned to Alden.

"It's not a place for the unwary," Alden said. "I've nearly been tripped up many a time. I agree with Jacob that there's no reason for fear if you're careful. But I also agree with the others that it's a place best avoided if you can possibly do so, because there are dangers within."

"No more than any other forest," Jacob insisted.

Timicin turned to Richard. "Just some sage advice to ponder."

"Those telling me the story said that there must be some enchantment at work. I was prepared to face that."

"No matter what you were told," Khalil said, "what you will face will be completely unexpected. We know. We've seen other men, as confident as you, taken aback by what they have endured trying to solve the riddle."

"If you're smart," Jacob called, "you'll turn around and go back to where you came from."

Richard smiled at him. "I've come too far to turn back now. Besides, I'm good at solving riddles. I've caught thieves that no one else could catch. Found missing lads and lasses that no one else could find. Turned up treasures that others thought were lost forever."

Gerasim reached over and patted Richard's arm. "Have at it then, friend."

Quentin returned to show Richard to a room.

When they were gone, Timicin put a leaf coin on the counter. "I say he'll last three days before giving up."

Deval put a leaf coin next to it. "Two."

Gerasim added to the coins. "Four."

Khalil set a leaf coin down. "I'm optimistic. Five."

Bennu sighed. "That leaves me with six or one."

Timicin turned to him. "You don't have to bet if you don't want to."

Bennu shrugged. "What's a leaf? One."

Alden felt strangely comforted. "They don't stay long?"

Timicin shook his head. "None of them do. The longest was, what, twelve days?"

"Eleven," Deval said.

"No one even came close to discovering the secret?" Alden asked.

"None," Timicin said.

"Most of us think this is the work of the Enchanters, and they guard their secrets carefully," Deval said.

That put Alden more at ease. He nodded.

When Quentin returned, the men gave them their coins for him to hold, pending the outcome. Matilda came out with the fish stew shortly thereafter.

When Jacob and Alden had finished their meal, they said their farewells and left the inn.

Once they were a few paces down the street, Jacob muttered, "Young fool."

"Yes, I was thinking about that while I was eating."

"Did anyone tell you what happened to the others who tried to discover the secret?"

"Only that they had failed."

"As Khalil said, Deval gave a lot of them the boot. Despite being warned, they thought that their trap, or their net, or their pit, or whatever, would work when everyone else's had failed. Some would sit and stare at the castle walls all night, and stagger in the next morning without seeing a thing. Deval had to fish some out of the river at the place where it meets the border of the forest."

"Drowned?"

"No, just waterlogged. Men would go into the forest and come out shivering so badly they couldn't hold a tankard if Quentin put their hands around one. Couldn't even tell us what happened in between. Said they couldn't remember anything except entering the forest. Others would wander down the street as if in a stupor...swore they never touched wine or beer."

"What do folks around here think happened to them?"

Jacob shrugged. "Most folks just say it's the Enchanters."

"What do you think?"

"I think that they just got scared and made excuses so others wouldn't think less of them."

Alden nodded. "I would believe that."

Jacob patted his arm. "You didn't come here to get a prize. That's what sets you apart...and everyone else who has fit in around here. Those that only come for a princess-prize leave just about as quickly as they come in."

* * *

When he settled into Jacob's house, Alden found that Jacob and Rose had a small library. Just a shelf, but Jacob seemed to enjoy reading by lamplight in the evening. After making some inquiries, Alden had found a bookstore and bought a few more books to add to the few he had always carried with him.

They were reading when they heard a pounding at the door. "Alden! Jacob!"

Jacob looked up. "That's Quentin. What could he want at this time of night?"

Alden put his book down. "I'll go see."

When Alden opened the door to the shop, he saw Quentin standing at the step with a lantern. "Alden, we need you to come."

"What is it?"

"That new man, Richard, seems to have taken a fall in the forest. He's calling for help, and those who heard him call out my name came to me, but I'd rather not go in there alone. I'll go in with you or Jacob, though."

"I'll come. Just let me go in and tell Jacob I'll be gone for a while."

As Alden had hoped, Jacob wanted to stay where he was. Quentin hurried to a place near the city limits where a small crowd had gathered.

"Won't someone just come in and help me." Richard sounded exasperated.

"We're here, Richard," Quentin said.

"Hand me the lantern," Alden said. "Follow right behind me and you should be all right."

Quentin nodded and gave Alden the lantern.

"Keep talking, Richard, so we can find you," Alden said.

"I'm here."

Alden held the lantern in front of him and picked his way through the grasses and around the trees.

"To your left," Richard called.

Alden turned and held the lantern.

Richard lay on the forest floor. "I tripped and this log rolled over my leg. I can't get it loose."

Alden put the lantern down. "Let's see what we can do." He and Quentin pushed the log out of the way. They helped Richard to his feet.

"Can you walk?" Quentin asked.

"I think I can," Richard said, and took a tentative step.

Alden took the lantern in one hand and grasped Richard's arm with his other. "You should stay between Quentin and I on the way out."

Quentin took the cue and grabbed Richard's other arm. He moved stiffly, so they walked slowly.

"How did you get here?" Alden asked.

"Quentin said I could get a view from the roof. When I looked, I saw a line of lights in the forest. I thought I would come and follow them to see where the line went."

"How close did you get?" Alden asked.

"The lights were gone when I reached the trees. I started in the direction I thought I saw them go, but as you see, I didn't get very far."

"If I can give a word of advice," Alden said, "I wouldn't go anyplace without getting your bearings first, especially to places you've never been before, particularly at night."

"Yes, I see that, but I was so sure...."

"Looks can deceive," Quentin remarked.

They reached the road without further incident.

The onlookers applauded briefly.

Richard scanned their faces. "Why didn't you come and help me? Why did you just stand here?"

A man stepped forward. "If we had gone in there, the same would have happened to us, and then we'd all need rescuing. We called Quentin for you, and he called Alden. You're out, safe and sound. Isn't that enough?"

Richard sighed.

Alden handed the lantern to Quentin. "Can you take him from here?"

Quentin nodded. "Thank you."

"Yes, thank you," Richard added.

Some of the onlookers dispersed. Others escorted Quentin and Richard as they walked away.

Alden walked through mostly empty streets to Juno's shop. A light was on. He knocked on the door softly. When it opened, he said to Juno, "I hope I'm not bothering you, coming this late."

"Not at all. Come in." She led him through the shop to a room with a couch and chairs. "I was just having tea. Can I pour you a cup?"

"Please."

As she walked to a table with a teapot, she gestured. "Please, have a seat."

When they each had a teacup in hand, Alden said, "I hope I won't offend if I ask a delicate question."

Juno smiled. "No, not at all. But I must warn you, I know very little. Probably not too much more than you."

"I saw you at the ball last night."

"Yes, I understand that you have eyes that see."

"And you?"

Juno reached for a box and set it on the table between them. The box was richly carved and elegantly ornamented with jewels. "Raven gave this to me before I went to my first ball. She said it was an Enchanter's gift. Did you see the buttons on my gown last night?"

Alden lifted his head slightly. "Yes. I don't usually notice buttons, but yours were unlike any I have ever seen before. They glowed like rare opals."

Juno nodded. "The buttons were inside this box. The day after the ball, we had customers come to the shop to tell us how delighted they were with their gowns, and that we should have been there to see them."

"They never saw you."

"They never noticed us. Either of us. Or, rather, they saw us, but did not recognize us."

Alden nodded. "The Enchanter's gift."

"Raven said there was already an enchantment masking her but needed one for me. I take it you had a similar gift?"

"Not buttons, but yes, a gift."

"Did you find it?"

"No, a man gave it to me. I think he was an Enchanter."

Juno lifted her chin. "I see. I think I know who."

"What are you free to tell me?"

"As I said, I know little more than you."

"My guess is that it's the child's father."

"That little I know, too."

"Why give the tokens to me?"

She spread her hands. "My guess, and it is only a guess, is that he wants you to perform some service for him."

"It would be useful if he explained what service he wants, in that event."

"I think he can't. The same as Raven can't. Or Philippa can't. I think they're bound by an oath."

He lifted an eyebrow. "That would fit with what I know."

She sighed. "I'll help you in any way I can, if I can. This double life of theirs needs to stop. I want a life with Raven. You want a life with Philippa. The child's parents want to be a family."

"I'll see what I can find out, as discreetly as I can. First, though, I have to deal with Richard."

"Richard?"

"The latest claimant to King Reginald's offer."

Juno laughed merrily. "I wouldn't worry about him, or any of them. They can't succeed. That's why the offer is so absurd. I wish His Majesty knew how absurd it is."

"Thank you. I'm at least comforted with that."

"You can set your mind at rest on that account."

Alden had been sipping tea during the conversation. He set the teacup and saucer down. "Speaking of rest, I'd better get back before Jacob starts to worry about me." He stood. "Thank you for the tea."

Juno rose. "I'll see you out." When they reached the front door of the shop, she added, "I don't plan to tell Raven about this conversation."

"I wasn't planning to tell Philippa, either. Good night."

Alden awakened to the sound of rain pattering on the roof. By now, he found the sound soothing rather than painful. In the time he had been in the realm, rain almost always came in the night and stopped by morning, but not this day. When he and Jacob opened the shop doors, the sky was still overcast, the gutters flowed with water, and drops fell from the edges of the roof.

He stood for a while under the shelter of the shop, looking out. The air remained mild despite the rain; he was not chilled. People hurried along the walks, heads covered with hoods or hats or coats. If the weather held through noon, he and Philippa would not meet for the midday meal. They had agreed earlier not to meet if the weather was inclement. Alden did not mind rain as long as he did not have to march in it, get his feet wet in it, get soaked by it. There had been far too many such days in his past. Now he had the luxury of staying away from it, and he did.

The rain did stop by the time they closed the shop. Jacob guided them through the forest on rocky paths and their boots remained largely clean and dry. The fish remained hungry as ever.

When Alden and Jacob walked in the door of Quentin and Matilda's with the fish, they saw a very happy Bennu sitting at the counter with a stack of coins in front of him.

"I won the bet," he said.

"Richard's gone?" Alden asked.

Bennu and the others nodded.

"All did not go well with the audience with the king and queen?" Alden said.

Quentin took the fish from Jacob. "Oh, he didn't even get that far. This morning, after breakfast, he offered to help Signe and I move beer kegs in the cellar. As we were working, Richard asked what happened when he married a princess? How would that work? Signe told him that he'd live in the castle as a prince, and when Reginald and Beatrice's reign ended, he and his wife would no longer be prince and princess but would have to find a home and employment outside the castle." Quentin smiled. "It was as if someone had struck him in the face. He asked, but wouldn't he be king? And Signe said no, the next ruler would be chosen by the Enchanters. He might try, but his chances would not be good."

"Did he finish helping you?" Jacob asked.

"To his credit, he did," Quentin said. "Then he went upstairs, packed his bags, paid his bill, and left."

"One of the city guard trailed him to the border, just to be sure," Deval added.

"Can he return?" Alden asked.

Deval shook his head. "You have to be born here or settled here to return. My guess is that you could return, Alden, but not Richard."

"I have no plans to leave. Even for a brief time. Ever," Alden said.

Deval slapped Alden on the back companionably. "And we are happy to have you here, Alden."

Quentin went to the kitchen with the fish. Jacob sat at his usual table. Alden joined him.

"Smart young woman, that Signe," Jacob said softly.

Alden nodded, musing that Princess Olympia had successfully spared herself a potential suitor.

Chapter 8

On Sunday, Alden and Philippa sat at their now-usual place on one of the stone benches around the city square. Ever since their first Sunday dance, they found that the crowd expected them to engage in at least one dance together, and often would gesture them to come and dance again. Both were more than happy to oblige.

Resting after a particularly complicated routine, they looked over the other dancers. Raven and Juno had partnered and had joined in among the couples.

Philippa indicated a black-haired woman leaning against a lamp-post, gazing eagerly at the assembly, swaying to the rhythm of the music. "Poor Sonia. She wants to join in so badly, but no one will ask her."

"Why not?"

"She's rather outspoken. Some young men her age want someone more demure."

Alden looked her over more closely. "Surely there must be someone among the young men who appreciates a young woman who will speak her mind."

Philippa nodded toward the dancers. "See the young man there with the long plume in his cap? That's Dimitri. Sonia has had her eye on him, but he hasn't noticed her."

"I take it word has gotten around?"

"I hear a lot at the coin exchange. You know how people talk."

"Hm." Alden rubbed his chin. "This isn't a royal ball, so I presume it wouldn't be considered uncouth to cut in? I've seen others do it at these Sunday dances."

"Oh, yes, people do it all the time. It's informal, like a parlor dance."

"I suppose I could cut in on Dimitri and deprive him of his partner."

"I'm not sure that Dimitri would then choose Sonia."

"When I was younger, when my sister and I couldn't get the partners we wanted, we'd start out dancing with each other, and then slide in on the partners we wanted and switch. We got remarkably good at it."

Philippa turned to Alden and looked him full in the face. "Yes! When we were younger, my sisters and I played a game at our parlor dances. We'd switch partners two or three times during the same dance, and so smoothly that the partners didn't have the time to protest. My father made a pretense of being annoyed, and when he did, we'd switch out his partners as well."

Alden grinned. "I knew that we were well matched."

Philippa smiled back and turned to the musicians. "This dance has ended. You take Sonia and I'll take Dimitri for the next dance." She stood, wiped her hands on her skirts, and then rubbed her hands together.

Alden walked over to Sonia and bowed. "May I have the honor of this dance, lady?"

Sonia beamed and curtsied. "I would be honored to accept, sir."

The musicians struck up a casual tune. Alden kept to simple steps and Sonia proved to be a more than adequate dancer. While maintaining polite attention on Sonia, he kept Philippa in view and gradually moved closer to her. When they were within arm's reach, he lightly grasped one of Sonia's hands and placed it on Dimitri's shoulder while Philippa took one of Dimitri's hands and placed it around Sonia's waist. Dimitri's other hand she put against Sonia's now-free hand. Philippa and Alden placed their hands in proper positions on each other and kept dancing.

As they had hoped, the rhythm of the dance kept Sonia and Dimitri together as the music played on. Looking back at the couple, Alden saw them smiling at each other. He turned to Philippa, who was also stealing glances at the younger couple.

"Success," Alden said to Philippa.

She smiled. "Yes."

Suddenly, Alden felt Philippa step to one side and release her grip. A moment later, he found himself facing Raven.

"You didn't tell me this was a change-partners dance," she said with a grin as she grasped his hand and side. "Juno and I thought if you could change with Sonia and Dimitri, we'd change with you and Philippa."

Turning, he saw Juno dancing with Philippa and laughing.

All this time, Alden had not missed a step. Now he changed his cadence slightly—though still in time with the music—and edged toward Philippa. When they were within reach, Alden released Raven. Philippa pulled her toward Juno and guided Juno into Raven's arms before rejoining Alden, who quickly moved them to a safer distance.

Before Juno and Raven could move back, the music stopped.

The onlookers applauded. Alden took Philippa's hand. They both bowed. Juno and Raven also bowed together.

Raven skipped toward Alden and Philippa. "That was fun! We haven't done that in years."

"I see you haven't forgotten," Philippa said with a sly smile.

"I thought only my sister and I did that," Alden said.

"Oh, no," Raven said, "we used to do that all the time."

"I must say that the rest of you did it so expertly that all I had to do was stand there," Juno added.

Raven took Juno's hand and faced her. "I'm sure I can teach you, if you're willing."

"More than willing," Juno said.

The music started again. Philippa took Alden's hand and turned to Raven. "Alden and I will sit this one out, I think."

Raven gave Philippa a knowing look and nodded solemnly.

While Alden wondered what that might be about, Philippa tugged at his hand. "Let's walk."

Alden bowed. "With you, to the ends of the earth."

She led him away from the city square to a garden spot within sight on the castle. They had the area to themselves, as was usual on a Sunday, when most gravitated to the city square.

Philippa let go of Alden and reached into a pocket. She brought out a gold chain which had a gold embossed disk attached to it. She placed it in his hand, then wrapped her fingers around his. "This is for you. If you ever need to go to the castle to talk to me, show this to the guard at the drawbridge. They will let you in. Our parents give similar ones to people they talk to during their walks through the streets if they want them to come back to the castle at a later date. Raven is giving one of her own to Juno."

He looked straight at her. "Is there a reason that I might have to go to the castle for you?"

"No reason I can think of now. But the future is uncertain."

"The future is always uncertain."

"I cannot but agree." She withdrew her hand.

He looked at the disk. It seemed to have a tiny hinge on the side, as if it were a locket. Opening it, he saw that each side contained a tiny portrait of Princess Electra. He closed the locket and put the chain around his neck, tucking the disk inside his shirt. "I will keep this close to my heart, as you are."

She reached over and put a hand on his cheek, then leaned forward and kissed him. He returned the kiss and put his arms around Philippa. She put her arms around him and drew him closer.

When their lips parted, she said, "I wish we could be handfasted, but since we cannot do that now, consider the locket to be a pledge."

"I will regard it as such."

That evening, after Jacob and Alden returned home from eating dinner at Quentin and Matilda's, Alden went to the wooden chest that Jacob had given him to keep his things in and drew out the cloak they had found near their fishing spot.

Jacob looked up from the chair he had settled in and lowered his book. "Meeting secretly with your sweetheart?"

Alden took a breath. "I thought I would take a walk in the woods."

"Good for you. There's nothing to be afraid of."

"Do you take walks in the woods? Other than fishing?"

He glanced upward a moment, as if gathering his memories. "Not recently. But when I was a lad of five, the other children would gather leaves from the trees at the edge of the forest. I tried, but by the time they had the leaves they wanted, there were none left that I could reach. My parents told me never to go into the woods, but I thought if I kept my house in sight, it would be all right.

"Before I could find an enchanted tree, I saw a tall man in nice clothes. I had no idea where he came from; he was just there all of a sudden. He crouched down to talk to me. He had a friendly face. He asked if I was looking for something, and I told him I was looking for leaves from the enchanted trees. He smiled and said that I must be looking for the trees whose bark seemed to sparkle. He said it was good to take the leaves from those trees because otherwise the trees would have to work hard to shed them and grow new leaves. He stood and pointed to trees nearby that had lots of leaves where I could reach them. He told me that I could come in any time. I said that a lot of people said not to come in the forest, that something bad might happen to them. He said that only those who came in to do mischief had anything to worry about. I went to get some leaves from the trees he pointed to, and when I turned to talk to him again, he was gone."

"Did your parents ever find out you went into the forest?"

"When I came home with a lot of slivers and an armful of leaves for us to use, my mother asked where I got them. Before I could answer, my father told her I must have gone to the Donner place and picked leaves from the trees by the donkey pens. He said he went there as a child because the other children were afraid the donkeys would bray at them or be nipped when the donkeys poked their heads through the spaces between the fence boards."

"They never found out?"

Jacob shook his head. "I just let them assume that."

"Did you tell your parents about the man?"

Jacob shrugged. "It never occurred to me to tell them about him. He was just a man."

"Your parents never told you not to talk to strangers?"

Jacob shifted his weight in the chair. "I've heard that from people who weren't born here. That children had to be warned or they would come to harm. That doesn't happen here. Children get lost, yes, but eventually they're found. My parents told me that if I was ever lost, I should just go up to someone and tell them I was lost."

Alden nodded.

"I wouldn't want to live where you came from. It sounds dangerous."

"Most people where I came from are good people. In my travels, more than once, when I was lost or hungry or injured, a complete stranger would take me in and help me, asking nothing in return."

"You never met anyone who was a threat?"

Alden inclined his head. "Many times. Besides my opponents in battle, there were raiders on the highways when I escorted merchants along the trade routes, and troublemakers at inns and such."

"What did you do?"

"Outside of battles, when it was my duty to meet our attackers, avoiding threats was the best option. After a time, I became pretty good at predicting when the atmosphere was getting tense and slipping away before words came to blows. When I couldn't do that, I would stand my ground and do my best to talk my way out. A lot of ruffians attack when they think others are weaker and will withdraw with a demonstration of strength or stubbornness. Others will retreat when given something they want, and I did when it was within my means to do so."

"And when that didn't work?"

"It almost always did. On rare occasions, I had to fight, and I am an experienced fighter. Most important, I found that often when one person shows the courage to fight, others will join your cause...enough so that the attacker becomes outnumbered and withdraws."

Jacob shook his head. "I would rather live here."

"I would, too."

Once cloaked, Alden carefully bypassed others on the streets and walks until he safely reached the woods overlooking the castle. As on the night of the ball, eventually he saw a tall man reach the castle walls and draw out the princesses. This time, Alden followed quietly at a distance. His task was made easier by the fact that all of them seemed to be encompassed by a soft glow.

As he walked along, Alden paid close attention to the path and his surroundings. He did not want to make a sound by stepping on a twig or snapping a branch. Though there was no moon in the sky, he would see everything clearly. Often, he would glance ahead at the backs of the walkers in front of him, to be sure they would not turn and spot him. None did.

Eventually the lights ahead became brighter. He could see that the leaves on the trees as he passed had turned to gold and silver. These trees were unlike any tree he had ever seen, not even resembling the trees at the edge of the forest where the children gathered their bounty.

The princesses slowed their pace, and Alden matched theirs. Now he could see tall marble buildings, also glowing. Looking up, he could barely see the tops of the spires. The treeline reached almost to the glistening marble flagstones surrounding the buildings. The princesses left the path and walked on the flagstones. Alden was about to do the same when an overwhelming feeling came over him, signaling him to stop. He did, right at the edge.

From his vantage point, he could see inside the building nearest him. There were no windows or doors, but a number of consecutive arches from ground to ceiling gave him a clear, unimpeded view.

The princesses seemed to be greeting a large group of tall people, dressed similarly to the man who led them. Alden presumed these were Enchanters. They appeared to be pleased that the princesses had arrived, and the princesses acted as if they were greeting old friends.

Now that he could see the Enchanters more closely, they seemed to be remarkably like any other people he had met in his travels, save that all were consistently taller than the princesses. There was a wide variety of hair colors and textures as well as variety of skin tones.

Alden stood far enough away that though he could hear voices, he could not make out words. Soon, the voices quieted, and he began to hear music. This was a pleasant sound, though it did not seem to originate from any instrument he had ever known. He did not see any musicians, though since he could not see the entire room, he presumed they could be out of view.

Everyone began to dance. He saw no one sitting out. Watching closely, he could see that some moves resembled other dances he knew, other moves were entirely novel. Partnered moves became line dances. At times they all moved the same, other times they wove between each other in a pattern. As the dance went on, he felt a...power...emanating from the room. He felt as if he were being buffeted by strong wind, though the air around him was calm.

He studied the dance closely for some time. Eventually, some gracefully detached from the main group of dancers and gravitated to the walls. One man wandered in his direction. Alden leaned back slightly but found he could not take a step in any direction. Fortunately, the man never turned to face him. Instead, he walked to a tree near Alden and stood with his back leaning against it, looking into the room. Now that he was closer, Alden recognized him as the one who had given him the ring. Since that night, Alden had never taken it off, and generally had forgotten about it—in fact, most of the time, he could not see it or feel it.

Meanwhile, the music had stopped. The dancers began to mingle and talk amongst themselves. Without turning his head, the man nodded and walked back into the room.

After a while, the music started again. Alden noticed it was the same dance. He lightly tapped the fingers of one hand against his thigh, keeping time with the music, which was also the same melody. This time he studied the dance moves with the thought of trying to learn it, imitate it.

By the time the music stopped again, Alden felt that he had a basic knowledge of the moves. Inside, the volume of talk rose again. Alden had the feeling that this was a farewell. He looked around, and this time his feet did move, and he was able to take a couple of steps inside the forest and shield himself from view behind a tree. The familiar man passed him on the path at a distance, followed by the princesses. While he waited for them to get ahead on the path, he gently plucked a gold leaf from the tree he was hiding behind, and a silver leaf from another tree within reach. The leaves yielded soundlessly to his touch.

Again, Alden followed at a distance until the princesses reached the castle. He turned and hurried to his usual vantage point and watched as the princesses entered again. Once the door in the wall had disappeared, the man leading them turned and disappeared into the forest.

Alden pocketed the leaves, took off his cloak, and folded it over his arm. The lamplighters had long since completed their work. He easily found his way back to Jacob's. When the clock in the city square sounded the hour, he turned. Only a couple of hours had passed. Surely he had been gone longer than that? Or perhaps not.

He found Jacob sound asleep as he came into the house and tread softly, putting the cloak away and tucking the leaves into his rucksack for safekeeping.

Alden debated as to whether he should tell Philippa of his nighttime discovery. This was decided for him when he met her at the coin exchange. After they shared a brief kiss, all thought of the night before left his mind, and he thought only of her and what the day had brought them. When escorting her back to the shop, he realized that he had said nothing about the previous night and felt this had been the best choice...for now.

That afternoon, when Jacob reached for the doors to close the shop and go fishing, he turned to Alden. "I told Sister Angelica that her lampstand would be ready by today, but she hasn't come. Would you go bring it to her? I'll close the shop and wait for you by the stream."

"Of course," Alden said. "But it may take me some time."

Jacob waved a hand. "Take all the time you need. The fish and I will be fine together, and Quentin won't fuss if we're late. I've done it before."

Alden grabbed the lampstand. "I'll meet you at the stream, then."

When he reached Sister Angelica's, he found that she had turned her ankle that afternoon and was resting. The other sisters escorted Alden to a receiving room, where he set the lampstand down and took her coins with thanks.

On the way home, he stopped at Juno's clothing shop, where she was just locking up.

"Can you delay a minute?" Alden asked.

She opened the door wider. "Yes. Come in, but I'll lock the door behind you."

When he was in the shop, he looked around. "Raven has gone home for the evening?"

"Yes."

He nodded. "I have a commission for you. I want you to sew me an outfit that a king might wear...or a prince."

She did not respond right away, staring at him with a strange expression.

"Is this not something you want to do?" he queried.

She waved a hand. "No...no, that isn't it. Stay here. I'll be back." Turning, she walked through the door at the rear of the shop and brought back a package wrapped in paper. Coming up to Alden, she drew the paper aside, showing rich woven cloth. "This was at the doorstep outside my living quarters this morning. No note, no instructions. Just there."

"Do you think it was there by chance?"

Her eyebrows went up, then down. "I'm beginning to think nothing relating to Raven and Philippa is by chance. I haven't told Raven about this."

"Can you sew me an outfit without her knowing?"

She nodded.

"Thank you." He reached into a pocket and brought out a branch coin. "Here's my first payment."

The shoe shop was also on his way back to Jacob's and the path to the stream. Alden stopped there, and again, found the proprietors just closing.

"Can you handle one more customer?" he called.

Jin turned to him and smiled. "Of course. Come in."

When they were seated facing each other, Alden said, "Those were excellent dancing shoes you made for me."

Jin nodded. "I make the best, if I do say so myself."

"Could you make me dancing shoes fit for a prince?"

He grinned. "Going to another ball?"

"Something like that."

He rubbed his chin. "You know, this morning, Li found a package of very fine, very supple, very tough material outside our shop. No writing on it. We examined everything and couldn't find a clue as to where it came from. Li said it must be a gift from the Enchanters. I was wondering what I could make with it."

"How about some shoes fit for a prince?"

"Such shoes would come at a higher price than the others I made for you."

"Name it."
He did. Alden paid.

The next night, and the next, and the next, Alden followed the princesses to the Enchanter palace. He carefully studied the dance, the rhythm, the timing. When he felt he had memorized the main steps, he turned his attention more to the hand and arm movements and other subtleties. Although the dance was always the same, the position of the dancers could and did change: sometimes the Enchanters were in one area and the princesses in another, sometimes they alternated, where an Enchanter would be next to a princess who would be next to another Enchanter. There seemed to be no difference in the gender of the dancer, the movements were identical.

Every night, the Enchanter who had given him the ring, whom he presumed was Lark's husband, came out of the palace to stand for a time near Alden. He never faced Alden, never spoke to Alden, never acknowledged Alden in any way except for the nod, which may or may not have been for him to observe. None of the other Enchanters or princesses showed any sign that they knew that Alden observed them. Philippa never mentioned or even hinted any sign of recognition of his nighttime presence at their midday meetings.

As the nights wore on, Alden found he was no longer frozen in position, though he remained hidden behind a tree next to the flagstones as he observed the dancers. He debated as to whether to put a foot on the floor and decided this was not the time.

Most of all, he consistently felt a surge of great potency emanating from the room, as invigorating as a fresh breeze on a warm morning. With such a feeling, he thought, he would have been willing to face an entire army on his own, armed only with a sturdy sword against a field of cannons and muskets. In response to the feeling of power, he straightened his back and squared his shoulders. His commanding officers would have found no fault with his posture.

After all of these excursions, he slept soundly and awakened feeling refreshed.

During the day, Alden kept up his work in the carpentry shop and fished with Jacob in the late afternoons. Jacob seemed to attribute Alden's nighttime journeys to a young man's need to work off excess energy before bedtime.

One day, when Jacob had gone to the back to relieve himself, one of the palace guards came into the shop in uniform. Alden recognized him as a man who had, days earlier, brought in a cradle and had given it to Jacob for repair. Since the cradle was ready, Alden grabbed it and brought it to the front of the shop.

As Alden set it down, the guard smiled. "It looks ready. My wife will be pleased."

"Congratulations."

The man nodded. "Due any day now." He reached into a pocket and counted coins into Alden's hand.

"Thank you," Alden said. "I didn't catch your name when you were last here."

"Silas. You must be Alden."

"I am."

Silas, a well-muscled man, lifted the cradle to chest level. "The castle folk are happy at the thought of having a baby around, at last. It's been a long time."

"You live in the castle?"

"My wife and I do, yes. Some of the guards live outside and rotate in and out, but we have rooms of our own."

"None of the other castle residents have children?"

"Older children, yes. No infants or toddlers for a long time. I know the queen and king have been hoping for grandchildren, but there will be none the way the princesses are going."

"What makes you say that?" Alden said pleasantly.

Silas tilted his head. "I know they're gone afternoons and evenings to who-knows-where. Probably up to no good."

"What makes you say that if you don't know where they go or what they do?"

Cradle still in hand, Silas shrugged. "Seems to me that secrecy tends to breed trouble."

"Not always. I couldn't conclude whether what they do with their time is good, bad, or indifferent. Tell me, since you are nearer to them than I am, in the time they are there, do they act courteously?"

Silas pressed his lips together, considering. "Yes, they do."

"Do you find fault in any of their behavior that you do know about?"

Again, Silas paused before answering. "No. No fault at all."

"Wouldn't it be more sensible to conclude, then, that they could be using their time constructively? Perhaps they're completing a task that they feel will delight and surprise their parents when it is revealed."

He appeared to be considering. "I hadn't thought of that."

Alden nodded back. "It is clear that the royal family values your service if they are as excited about your and your wife's happy event as you are."

Silas tilted the cradle briefly in Alden's direction. "I had heard that you were fair spoken, friend. I see that what I heard was true."

"I am humbled by their high opinion of me."

Silas swung around toward the castle. "I hope we meet again, friend."

"May it be sooner rather than later."

Chapter 9

Eventually, the shoes and the outfit were finished. Alden tried on the shoes at Jin's. They fit perfectly. As Jin put them in a box, Alden praised the craftsmanship.

Jin nodded. "Best shoes I've ever made. Wear them well."

When he reached Juno's, she showed him the shirt, jacket, and pants before he tried them on. "The stitches all but disappeared after I put them in. There was no fraying of the cloth, either."

Alden nodded. "The cloth truly was enchanted, then." He went behind the screen, changed, and emerged.

Juno took in the effect. "I sewed largely in the evenings, by lamplight. The cloth glows, though it's difficult to tell in the daytime."

Standing in front of the mirror, he examined the embroidery. "This is outstanding. I have not seen princes in my travels better arrayed."

He went back behind the screen and changed again.

Juno folded the outfit carefully, wrapped it in paper, and tied it with a string. "Are you going tonight?"

Alden nodded.

"I'm afraid for you. What will they do if they notice you?"

"I admit to some foreboding, but there's no record of an Enchanter killing anyone, so what could they do?"

"I don't know. That's what bothers me." She put a hand on his arm. "Promise me you'll knock on my door when you return. Whatever the hour."

"I promise."

"May the blessings of heaven go with you."

"Thank you."

Alden put the packages in Jacob's house before joining him at the stream. When they reached Quentin and Matilda's inn, he noticed some of the regulars looking at him with a strange expression.

"Someone else came in from outside?" he guessed.

"No," said Bennu with a smile. "We think someone has marriage on his mind and has been getting an outfit ready."

"You know how people talk," Quentin said.

Alden inhaled as his mouth formed a silent "Oh." Of course the townspeople would have noticed his comings and goings at Juno's shop.

"When's the occasion?" Khalil asked.

"And are we invited?" Gerasim said.

Alden waved a hand. "There's no date yet. When there is, of course you'll be invited."

"How about the lucky bride?" Deval asked. "Is she getting ready?"

"I have the impression that the lucky bride has inherited quite a trousseau and needs no preparation in that area," Alden said.

"Always nice when the bride has a dowry," Bennu said.

"It is," Alden said.

"Just don't leave me alone," Jacob said.

"Jacob," Quentin said, "you can't expect...."

Alden cut him off with a gesture and placed a reassuring hand on Jacob's shoulder. "Jacob, nothing's going to happen right away. I said you won't be left alone, remember?"

Deval looked around at his companions, taking them in. "Of course you won't be left alone, Jacob. You have all of us to count on."

"That is true, Jacob," Quentin said. "You can count on all of us."

Jacob seemed reassured and sat at his usual spot at the table.

That evening, as he walked toward the royal castle, cloaked, Alden reflected that he had been less nervous on the eve of battle. He kept reminding himself that there had never been a report of an Enchanter hurting anyone, much less killing anyone. Even Nevarth, one of their own who had betrayed them, had been dealt with by exile. Alden felt that exile could be the worst possible result. Given his history of being unnerved by even moderate noise, however, death might even be preferable. Somehow that thought strengthened his resolve: nothing they might do could be worse than what he had already lived through.

Meanwhile, as he did before battles, he put all thoughts of possible misery out of his mind and concentrated on the task at hand. As usual, he followed the princesses to the Enchanters' palace. He stood behind a tree while the dance started. Long before, he had determined which part of the dance would present its greatest opportunity. He kept time to the music, estimating where in the melody he would need to start to get to the dance floor at the correct moment.

When it came, he acted quickly. Lark's husband happened to be paired with Electra at that moment. Alden removed his cloak, strode across the flagstones into the room, pulled the Enchanter away, took Electra's hand, and continued with the dance. No one made a move to stop him, no one voiced a protest.

The music and dance continued. He knew every step: when to weave, when to change partners, when to dance alone. The others became blurs to his eyes, the walls all but invisible, but he attended to the tune until it stopped.

He stopped. He felt dizzy. Two strong hands clutched his right forearm. Without that support, he would have toppled over.

A mighty hand clapped his left shoulder. "Well done, sir," said a voice. He was firmly embraced and released.

The strong hands kept their grip on his forearm.

Eventually, his vision cleared. He found himself facing a line of Enchanters staring directly at him. Now that he was close and had the time to study them, the one feature that stood out was that none of them had wrinkles, or moles, or pock marks, or any irregularity on their skin.

He took a breath and dared steal a glance to his right. Princess Electra held on to his arm with a determined look on her face.

He turned his attention back to the Enchanters.

An Enchanter, a woman, spoke. "That was unexpected."

Alden felt a nudge from behind. Looking back and forth quickly, he found he was surrounded by princesses, all facing the Enchanters as if daring the Enchanters to challenge them.

Lark's husband faced the speaker, then extended his arm to the princesses. "Mother, this is my bride, Lark."

Lark stepped forward and took her husband's hand.

Another Enchanter, a man, standing beside the woman who had spoken, turned to the Lark's husband. "Are you telling us, Elenath, that you and Lark are married?"

"Yes, Father, I am," he said. "She is also the mother of our child."

"We have a grandchild?" said the woman.

"Yes," Elenath said.

"You have kept our grandchild from us?" said the woman.

"Do you realize what you have done?" the man said.

"Yes," Elenath said. "I have started a family. I intend to keep my vows, as a husband and a father."

The man gestured to Lark. "You have ruined this woman's life!"

"Not true, Sherian," Lark said. "Elenath has not ruined my life. The oath that you required of us has ruined my life...our lives. Otherwise, we would have a nice house in the valley and live openly like any other family in this realm...Enchanter or not."

"You know why we required an oath from you," the woman said kindly.

"Yes. We saw the necessity and we took it," Lark said.

"And now it is time for that to end," Elenath said.

"The danger has not ended," Sherian said.

Elenath released Lark and shouldered his way through the princesses until he stood behind Alden. He put both hands on Alden's shoulders. "This man is our key. He is not bound by any of our oaths. He is free to move as he wishes."

Alden wondered whether to feel flattered or conscripted. He unquestionably felt alive, whole, and on his feet. In the Enchanter's palace. To him, that was a victory, whatever else happened.

"But he has no knowledge," the woman said, "and without knowledge, he cannot truly take part. We cannot give him that knowledge unless he is bound by an oath."

"Nonsense, Lunaria," Electra said. "Taking an oath seemed wise at the time you presented it. But that time has passed.

The oath is more of an impediment than a help. In your heart, you must know that."

"For my part," Alden said, finding his voice, "I am taking no oaths here and making no promises. You will have to trust my integrity."

"I examined him thoroughly as he approached our realm," Elenath said. "Nevarth has never touched his mind. He has never seen Nevarth; Nevarth has never seen him. I have watched him closely and he has always acted with honor. I trust him."

"Speaking for my sisters, we trust him," Electra said.

Behind him, Alden heard murmurs of agreement.

Lunaria and Sherian turned to other Enchanters. "Zara, Wessalor, what do you think? You have the most experience with the world outside."

Two Enchanters glided toward them...at least, it seemed to Alden that they glided.

One, a woman, stopped in front of Alden and looked him in the eye. "First, let's allow this man to sit. Bring out some furnishings. Get some water for him."

"How about some wine?" Princess Vinia suggested.

"No, it'll go to his head."

Somehow, chairs and couches were produced. Alden sat on a couch, leaning back. Electra sat next to him. She released his arm.

The woman, presumably Zara, sat across from him and leaned toward him. "You did well for someone here the first time. Those from outside find the magic overwhelming until they're used to it."

An Enchanter handed Electra a cup. She passed it to Alden. He drank, realizing that he was, actually, thirsty. He felt better after draining it. He held the empty cup in his lap.

"Is your mind clear enough to listen to an explanation?" Zara asked.

Alden nodded. "I've been in worse shape after a battle."

"I don't doubt it." Zara leaned back a little. "To come directly to the matter, our numbers have slowly dwindled through the years. That's the reason we opened our realm—carefully—to those from outside. At first, it was because there were not enough of us to work the land. But Nevarth remained a threat. You've heard of Nevarth?"

"Yes."

"Ever since we exiled him, Nevarth has regularly gathered armies to attack us. In his most recent attacks, we have barely repelled him. We needed more strength. After discussion, we decided we would approach our neighbors here who might be willing to help us."

"The princesses."

"Yes. They were willing. It did take time for them to accustom themselves to our magical surroundings, as you are. It took time for us to weave our magic into a form that they could use, or at least, channel."

"The dance."

"Yes. But we felt it was vital that Nevarth not know. We bound the princesses with an oath not to reveal what they were doing. We found that Nevarth sensed something different happening among us. He began to touch the minds of outsiders seeking us to observe and report what they saw in this realm or touch their minds if they left. Not all, of course. But we had to deny entry to some of those outside who could have made good additions to our realm because they had seen or been seen by Nevarth."

Alden thought of the family that he had encountered on the way in. They seemed to him like decent folk, but perhaps Nevarth had touched their minds. He nodded.

"Of course," Electra said, "Father began to notice our absences. We already were under strict supervision growing up, and we had already found out how to use the castle's enchantment to allow us to leave during the day and get on with our lives."

"...which is how the Enchanters found us to make their proposal in the first place," Rhea added.

"When we started disappearing in the night as well," Electra continued, "and coming home with worn shoes, there were words between us. Since we couldn't explain ourselves, Father sent out news with our merchants who traded at the nearby towns that anyone solving the mystery would get one of our hands in marriage."

"That, in itself, would not have been too bad," Lydia said. "I felt it was not much different than getting a husband using a matchmaker."

"Except that he first announced the proposal in the castle," Electra said, "and the castle's enchantment bound him to give one of our hands in marriage to anyone who revealed what we were doing. But since we couldn't reveal what we were doing, and the Enchanters wouldn't allow anyone who might be touched by Nevarth to find out, the riddle might never be solved."

"The oaths were binding us too tightly," Elenath said. "So I waited to find someone with integrity, not bound by any oath, who could help us. None of us could tell you directly, of course, you had to find out by yourself."

Zara turned to Elenath. "He had a little help."

"Yes, but I never broke the oath," Elenath said.

"Couldn't you freely move about the city?" Alden asked. "Probably no one could tell you were an Enchanter."

"Nevarth would know," Wessalor said. "He could touch the minds of anyone who might have seen us."

"Nevarth is coming to the end of his life," Zara said. "We all do, eventually. He seems to be single-mindedly determined to ruin us before he goes. Since you have arrived, we have, in fact, repelled one attack by a substantial army."

Alden opened his mouth to reply, then shut it as a memory flooded in.

Electra leaned toward him. "What is it?"

"The last town I visited before I came here," Alden said. "There was a group of men, gathering men-at-arms for a powerful general, they said. I've seen many such groups in my time. They gave a speech to those at the inn where I was staying, telling the men there that anyone who joined that the plunder would be great and the battle would be easy because those in the country to be attacked were but sheep. Every man would become a lord and the people of the country would be their vassals."

"That sounds like Nevarth," Wessalor said.

Alden turned to him. "They said that the general would come by the end of the month with those he had gathered at other towns, so I didn't see him, as Elenath said. Since I wasn't interested in joining, I simply ate my meal in the common room and went to my bed."

The Enchanters looked at him with rapt attention. "Yes, those men were surely part of the army with Nevarth that we repelled," Wessalor said.

"The dance worked," Alden said.

"To our great relief, yes," Zara said. "There has been a lull, and we've let in a few carefully selected people, but another attack is inevitable. After spending his waning strength in gathering his most recent army, he can no longer lead such a massive force against this realm. But he can cause great havoc here by himself... not among us, but among our friends here. We are no longer strong enough to prevent Nevarth from slipping in undetected."

"What could he do?" Alden asked.

"The greatest danger is that he could use the elements to harm or destroy," Wessalor said. "Lightning, winds, floods. He can cause panic or fear. His power of persuasion is strong but not absolute, and takes time, but still, he can influence single persons to do his bidding, especially those he catches unprepared for his deceptions."

"If you can repel an army, why can't you repel one individual?" Alden asked.

"For the same reason it is easier for one spy to slip past a blockade than it is for an armada to do so," Wessalor said.

"It is, again, a matter of numbers," Zara said. "We no longer have the numbers to keep out one of our own."

"Individuals or small groups without magic we can still keep out easily, of course," Elenath said.

"And the dance, the magic within the dance, now has the power to oppose him," Zara said.

"Or anyone else outside who might get an idea to wreak havoc among us," Elenath said.

"This is why we still need to keep this a secret," Wessalor said. "We can no more predict the exact moment that Nevarth will finally expire than we can predict the exact moment of our own deaths. But as Zara said, he has been expending a great deal of his strength trying to attack us, and that strength is quickly waning at the end of his life. It may be a matter of just a few years more."

"We hope," Elenath said.

Alden gradually began to feel more clear-headed. An idea came to him. "With your permission, I could join the dance nightly."

Zara nodded. "That would be welcome. You did well to come here with the clothing you did. Our clothing seems to lessen the shock of being surrounded by magic for the first time."

"If I may say so, I observed your dances for days before I walked in."

Everyone around him looked startled, except Elenath.

"I helped a little with that," he said.

"Alden is not afraid of the forest," Rhea said. "I presume that also helped."

Electra turned to Alden. "As with everyone else on the non-magical side of the realm, we were warned about the forest since we were children. It's true that the enchantment guards the forest against those who wish to do harm. It is also true that as one draws near to this place, and begins to feel the power, the mind unused to magic can become confused."

Alden nodded. "That would explain a lot of the mishaps."

"We have told and do tell our friends that the forest needs to be approached with caution," Zara said. "And we rescue them discreetly if no other help arrives."

An Enchanter approached Zara and gave her a package, nodding at Alden as he did so.

Zara gave the package to Alden. "Here is another set of clothes for you."

Alden pulled back the wrappings slightly. "Will they fit?"

Good-natured chuckling from the assembly answered him.

"They'll fit," Zara said with a smile.

"Can I keep on wearing these clothes?" Alden asked.

"Of course," Zara said. "But it's best to have more than one set of clothes, don't you agree?"

Electra reached over, placing a hand on the package. "If you don't mind, I can keep this safely at the castle until you call for it."

Alden gave her the package. "Thank you. It'll save me the time and trouble of finding a space at Jacob's for yet another set of clothes."

As Alden and Electra were speaking, Lunaria approached Elenath and Lark. "I want to see my grandchild."

Sherian took Lunaria's hand. "We want to see our grandchild."

"We do not have your talent for stealth, son," Lunaria said.

Lark turned to Elenath. "Would it be safe to bring her here?"

Elenath took Lark's hands in his. "I can feel the magic within her. Yes, she will be safe coming here. She's partly mine, after all."

Lark turned to Lunaria. "She's still an infant. Can you find a nurse for her? I'm afraid I'm past nursing."

Lunaria stepped forward and put a hand over Lark's. "My dear. We have magic. Of course you can nurse her, if you wish. We can arrange for nursing here, in your absence."

"Thank you," Lark said. "I'll tell the foster mother that Elenath will come for her. She knows him on sight and knows he's her father."

"Speaking of leave-taking, it is time," Elenath said.

The princesses and Alden all rose from their seats.

Alden bowed deeply to the Enchanter assembly. "I am honored by your trust in me."

Zara turned to him. "We are not without the means to verify that trust."

"Or to act quickly if the trust is broken," Wessalor said.

"If you cannot trust my integrity, trust my will to live. I came here because I truly had no where else to go and could not have lived longer outside. This realm is my last and only home." He turned to Electra. "If you can't trust those, trust my heart. It is given to Electra, and I cannot imagine life away from her."

Electra squeezed his hand. Alden turned to her, taking both of her hands in his. He leaned toward her; she leaned toward him until their foreheads touched. They exchanged a smile as their fingers intertwined. Then they separated and turned back to the Enchanters.

"The feeling seems to be mutual," Zara said.

"Can you read our thoughts?" Alden asked.

Zara took a breath. "We can read your...I think you call it 'nature.' We can read your passions and your feelings. Most of all, we can glimpse what you have seen. But your thoughts? No."

"The assurances you have given us are strong," Wessalor said. "That is something we can discern."

* * *

Alden separated from the princesses at the castle, after gallantly kissing Electra's hand in farewell. He immediately walked to Juno's, knocked at her door, and waited. After a few minutes, he wondered how long he should wait. But the door, at last, opened. Juno motioned him inside.

When she had closed and locked the door behind him, she faced him. She wore a long robe and slippers. "I tried to keep watch but fell asleep. I'm sorry for the wait. I cannot tell you how relieved I am to see you. How did it go?"

Alden smiled. "All is well."

Juno sighed. "Thank you for coming to tell me."

"Of course. I do have a word for you."

"Which would be?"

"Ask Raven to teach you the dance. She'll know what you're referring to." Alden did not know whether Juno would, or could, join them at the Enchanter's castle. Aside from having to get used to the magic, gaining the trust of the Enchanters seemed to be a difficult task. But Juno's heart was joined to Raven's, and she needed to be a part of Raven's task, as he was to Philippa's.

Another thought occurred to Alden. "Oh, and do you have any of that cloth left?"

"I do."

"Make a gown for yourself. Fit for a princess."

In the days that followed, Alden walked to the Enchanter Castle every night with the princesses, this time openly. He quickly became accustomed to the magic there. He wore the enchanted clothes, kept the ring Elenath had given him, and even tucked the leaves he had plucked in an inside pocket of an undershirt, near to the locket Electra had given him. Unlike the princesses, his shoes, made of enchanted materials, did not wear out.

Lunaria and Sherian's joy overflowed when Elenath and Lark brought the baby. If Alden had ever held the belief that the Enchanters were stoic and aloof, that belief dissolved at the sight of the Enchanters surrounding the baby, cooing and grinning as elders anywhere did at the sight of an infant. For her part, Astra gurgled happily, enjoying all the attention.

They danced, of course. No one ever found fault with Alden or corrected him, so he presumed that all of his moves were accurate. He asked Electra about his performance on the way back to the castle one night. She affirmed that everything about his participation was properly done.

It was not only the magic that overwhelmed him in the early days. The strength of the power he felt during the dance gave him the reassurance that nothing could withstand it, not even a rogue Enchanter.

Since his arrival, the weather had not troubled him. But one day, as he and Philippa walked hand-in-hand from the city square toward the coin exchange after the midday meal, he saw distant lights flashing over and beyond the mountains, and a sound that reminded him of far-off cannon fire. This did not unnerve him, as it had in the past, but it did worry him. He stopped to look and listen.

Nodding in that direction, he asked Philippa, "Have you seen these lights and sounds before?"

She followed his gaze. "Lightning and thunder? Yes. Just a storm beyond the mountains."

"How often do you see a sight like that?"

She paused before answering. "Not often. The rains and winds here tend to be soft. I've heard reports of violent tempests in other lands from those not born here, though."

That evening, between dances, he approached Zara and asked about what he had seen.

"Yes, what you observed today was not ordinary weather," she said. "That storm was a reflection of Nevarth's moods. We sense that he is coming closer. We will do what we can keep him at a distance as long as we have strength but it is still possible that he might slip in undetected by us. Nonetheless, if he comes here, we ought to be able to discover him quickly enough and counter any measures he might use."

Alden did not feel entirely reassured.

Chapter 10

The following Sunday, Alden and Philippa were dancing happily with the crowd when a shadow fell across the city square. At first, Alden felt it was just a cloud passing in front of the sun and thought nothing of it. Then the couple dancing next to him stopped and looked up. Others followed suit. One by one, the musicians stopped playing. The dancing stopped. All eyes turned upward to see a huge ominous cloud, glowing red at the edges, where moments before a clear sky with a few small white clouds had reigned.

Alden looked around. Others murmured in low voices. He glanced around and saw Jacob, sitting on a stone bench, peering upward.

Philippa drew closer to Alden. "Have you ever seen anything like that before?"

"Twice in my travels I've seen clouds that I felt were harbingers of doom. The elders among us said they were naught but clouds, and nothing untoward happened, but I think this one might be different."

Philippa nodded. "I don't think it's a natural cloud, either."

Juno and Raven approached them. "What is it? Shall we do something?" Raven said in a low voice.

Alden took Philippa's hand. "Let's do the dance."

"Here?"

"The dance itself isn't secret or sacred, as I understand."

"I agree with Alden," Raven said. "It should do no harm, and it may do a bit of good."

"It may make people dizzy, that's all," Alden said.

"No," Philippa said, "that comes from the enchantment in the palace, not the dance itself."

"Then there is no reason not to try," Alden said.

Philippa got into position to start. Juno and Raven reached out to each other. The four of them began to dance. At first, they were surrounded only by silence. Then the musicians struck up a tune, the same tune they danced to in the Enchanter's palace.

"How do they know that?" Alden asked Philippa.

"The dance provides its own tune," Philippa explained. "They probably hear it in their heads."

Moments later, the onlookers began to clap in time.

As the dance went on, the day seemed to become brighter. Alden glanced up to see the cloud shrinking and the sky turning blue again. By the time the dance ended, the cloud had gone.

The onlookers applauded and cheered.

The four dancers bowed and waved to the crowd.

"Four seems to be enough to make a difference," Alden said, "though I doubt it would be enough to drive away an armed force."

"At least we lightened the mood," Raven said.

Alden looked up briefly. "That's not all we lightened."

"Was it just a cloud?" Juno asked.

"There's a feeling in my bones that it was something more," Alden said.

"I felt the same way," Raven said.

The musicians started a new, familiar tune and their audience became dancers again.

The four of them stepped away from the crowd.

"I want to ask the Enchanters about this," Alden said in a low voice. "Now. I presume we aren't forbidden to seek them out?"

"They never have forbidden it," Philippa said.

"We'll go with you," Raven said.

Alden held out a hand. "No. I want you to help Juno pack her necessities and admit her to the castle so that she's safe in case there is something amiss."

Raven opened her mouth, closed it, and opened it again. "Yes. I'd have to slip into the castle first, and Juno would have to ask for admittance at the drawbridge."

"There's an empty room next to the castle seamstress," Philippa said.

"Will she object to another seamstress in the castle?" Alden asked.

"No," Raven said. "She just does mending. Dressmaking and tailoring are done by others, including Juno and me." Raven turned to Juno. "She is a talker, however."

Juno shrugged. "I don't mind. I had a favorite uncle who I swear could talk from sunup to sundown. And the less I have to talk, the better I can keep our secrets."

Raven and Juno took each other's hand and walked away.

Philippa took Alden's hand. They made their way to the forest. Before entering, Alden looked around to be sure they were not being observed and up to be sure that the cloud had not reappeared.

Philippa led the way. She seemed sure of the direct route, and they had entered the forest at a point that Alden was unfamiliar with. When they had walked what Alden reckoned was at least a half mile, Philippa stopped.

Alden turned to her. "Are we near the castle?"

"No. But we cannot go farther."

Alden furrowed his brow, and stepped forward, only to be met by a barrier. He could not see it, but he contacted something gently unyielding from his toes to his chin.

He stepped back. "I haven't encountered anything like this before."

"Nor have I."

"Can we see if we can feel our way around it?"

Philippa and Alden thrust their hands forward and tried to feel their way along the invisible wall.

After a few minutes, Philippa stopped and shook her head. "We're going away from the Enchanter's castle, not toward it."

"Are the Enchanters prisoners, I wonder?" Alden said.

"Perhaps they feel a need to keep us out for a time, for safety," Philippa said.

"Nevarth," Alden said.

Philippa nodded.

"Maybe he slipped the barrier," Alden said. "In that case, they're better equipped to handle him than we are."

"True, but I remain uneasy," Philippa said.

Alden nodded. "As do I." He took a deep breath and let it out. "I suppose we have no choice but to go about our business."

Philippa nodded back. "Come to the castle at the usual time. Perhaps Elenath will be there."

After separating from Philippa, Alden walked back to the city square. Jacob remained seated at the stone bench but looked up when Alden approached.

"Are you going out again tonight?" Jacob asked.

"Yes."

"Couldn't you stay in at least one night? I don't want to be alone tonight."

"How about staying at Quentin and Matilda's?"

"It's too noisy once the suppertime crowd arrives, and they're noisy until late."

Sister Angelica approached them at this moment. "Many I have talked to want a gathering of prayer and meditation this evening. We each would pray in our own way, of course. The convent garden will be open. You're welcome to come if you wish."

Alden turned to Jacob, who had stood when Sister Angelica approached. "Why not go there? You won't be alone, and it will be quiet."

Jacob shook his head.

Sister Angelica smiled. "There's still a common room at the residences where men get together to play cards every night. You spent a lot of time there before marrying, as I recall. As when you were younger, there are cots along the wall where the card players sleep between or after games. Your usual bed is probably in the same place."

Jacob seemed to consider for a few moments, then turned to Alden. "Can't you stay for just one night?"

Before Alden could answer, Sister Angelica said, "The heart must follow its lead. As you did with Rose."

Jacob rubbed his nose. "I suppose I could come."

"You may even recognize some of your old companions there," Sister Angelica said. "They have not forgotten you."

Jacob rubbed his nose again and took a long breath. His expression softened. He nodded.

Alden patted his arm. "Let's get together a few necessities for you. I can bring some fish to Quentin and Matilda."

"There will be a good spread at the residences tonight," Sister Angelica said. "You and Alden can eat there."

"I'll fish with Alden, then come to eat and play cards," Jacob said.

"Thank you for your invitation," Alden said, "but I'll have fish stew at Quentin and Matilda's tonight before going out."

Sister Angelica smiled at him.

Even though they had gone fishing earlier than usual, the fish still bit. When they got back to Jacob's house, Alden placed the fish in their usual basket while Jacob put a few things of his in a sack.

Alden made sure that Jacob was settled at the residence building before leaving for Quentin and Matilda's. The card players spotted Jacob as he walked through the door and greeted him warmly. They told him they were going to dinner after their current hand was complete. Jacob put his sack on a cot and made himself at home.

The card players invited Alden to join them for dinner. He politely declined and took the basket to Quentin and Matilda's. When he entered and closed the door behind him, Quentin said, "Where's Jacob?"

"At the residence next to the convent. He seemed unsettled after the cloud this afternoon."

"Who wasn't?" Gerasim said.

"Sister Angelica said there's a community prayer service in the convent garden."

"Good idea," Bennu said.

Alden handed the basket of fish to Quentin.

Deval turned to Alden. "You missed the next king of the realm."

"Who?" Alden asked.

"Someone came in from the outside," Timicin said. "Tall man, richly dressed. Merchant, maybe."

Tall.

"Where is he now?" Alden asked.

"That was strange about him," Deval said. "He was interested in the princesses, but he seemed more interested in the cloud this afternoon. He asked how it had been dispersed."

"We told him we didn't know," Khalil said, "but that after you and Philippa and Juno and Raven danced, it went away."

"Then he asked about you," Deval said, "all of you."

"What did you tell him?" Alden asked.

"We said that you should be coming here soon, if he would just wait," Deval said. "But he said it was important he see you right away. I said you were in the carpentry shop facing the city square, but he said he'd already been there and the shop was closed."

"Yes, we closed it when I took Jacob over to the residences."

"We told him where Juno's shop was, too," Gerasim said. "We don't know where Philippa and Raven live. We presume out in the country someplace, and they come in for the day."

Quentin returned from the kitchen. "You talking about that fellow that came in?"

The regulars nodded.

Alden faced them. "Do you trust me?"

They looked from one to the other. Deval said, "Of course we do, Alden."

Alden felt it would be unwise to tell them about Nevarth, but he needed to caution them nonetheless. "This man that came in, he sounds like some of the men I encountered in my travels. Obsessed with magic. Wants to find out all the so-called secrets. He could create a lot of damage trying to get what he wants."

"Would the Enchanters let someone like that in?" Quentin mused.

"I think that cloud had something to do with the Enchanters. Maybe this fellow slipped in. I'm going to the palace to talk to the king and queen. If this man comes here again, delay him. Tell him you have information he needs."

"What are you going to do?" Quentin asked.

"Warn the king and queen so that the princesses will be wary of this man."

"Do you need me to go with you?" Deval said.

"No, I need you, especially you, to be here to detain the man if you see him again." Alden walked to the door.

"Best of luck, Alden," Quentin called after him, and the others did the same.

Alden hurried to the castle. He did not run, thinking that might attract attention, but he rushed. As he did so, he reckoned as best he could. If Nevarth went looking for him and the others at Jacob's and Juno's, it would be a while before he could walk back to the inn, and even longer to the castle. That is, if Enchanters moved at the pace of everyone else. Everything he observed seemed to say that they did. Or perhaps he had a horse.

He put those thoughts out of his mind as he drew near the drawbridge. Silas was among the guards.

"Well met, Silas," Alden said. "Any news of the young one?"

Silas turned to face him and smiled. "A boy. We named him Matthew."

"And your lady?"

"Very well, thank you."

Alden reached inside his shirt for the chain, drawing it over his head and opening the locket. "The Princess Electra gave me this. I need to talk to her and Their Majesties right away."

Silas reached over and touched the locket, though he did not take it away from Alden. "Yes, it looks genuine."

"Her Royal Highness said this would admit me."

"Yes, but they're at dinner right now. Perhaps in an hour."

Alden took a breath. "It's important that I speak to them right away."

"Why?"

"It's a matter of great importance."

"I'm listening."

"Have you found me to be a man of honor?"

"Yes, of course."

"Can you trust me on this? It is for their ears only."

Silas turned to the guards next to him, who shrugged.

Alden reached into his inside pocket and drew out the gold and silver leaves. "I have solved the riddle of the princesses. Surely His Majesty would want to hear this without delay."

Silas reached out and felt the leaves Alden held out. Again, he turned to his companions.

"I don't know about you, but I would want to hear this," said one.

Silas withdrew his hands and nodded. "Come with me."

Alden suppressed a sigh of relief and followed. They had gone through a very long corridor when Silas turned a corner. When Alden turned the same corner and looked ahead, Silas was not there.

Alden stopped and cursed his luck. He remembered what Deval said about people regularly getting lost in the castle. He turned around quickly, but no one was there to ask.

He considered his choices. The room where the royal family dined could not be behind him or Silas would have stopped. He proceeded ahead until he came to an intersection. Neither direction seemed to appeal to him. He took a step to his right, and felt the same urge to stop as he had the first night near the Enchanters' palace. Taking a step to the left seemed easier. He continued on his way and heard voices and music through an open door.

Stepping inside, he saw a large room, lavishly decorated. A long table had been placed close to one of the walls. The king and queen sat in the middle and the princesses were evenly divided on either side.

Musicians had been playing in a corner but stopped when Alden entered. Everyone turned to him. Alden took note of where Electra and Raven sat. He also noted that Nevarth was not there...yet.

Alden bowed deeply. "Your Majesties, your pardon, but my errand will not wait."

"What is it?" Reginald asked.

"I have solved the riddle of the princesses."

Reginald turned to his daughters, who smiled, and motioned Alden to a place across the table opposite him

"You did not seem interested in discovering this secret when I spoke with you at the ball," Reginald said.

"I was not at that time," Alden said, "but times have changed, and I found it urgent to do so."

"Then tell us," Beatrice said.

He faced Reginald and Beatrice. "Every evening, your daughters leave the castle by magic, under escort from an Enchanter. They travel to the Enchanters' city in the enchanted forest, where they perform a magical dance taught to them by the Enchanters. The purpose of the dance is to repel Nevarth, who again brought armies to threaten this realm. The Enchanters no longer had the number to repel him with their magic, and the princesses were willing. So that Nevarth would not discover this, the princesses were bound by an oath not to reveal what they did at night to anyone. That is why they have not been able to tell you."

Reginald and Beatrice looked at their daughters, who looked back but said nothing.

Reginald turned back to Alden. "Do you have proof of this?"

Alden stepped forward and handed him the leaves. "Leaves from the trees in the Enchanters' city."

Reginald examined the leaves, passed them to Beatrice, then nodded at Alden.

"One more boon I would ask, Your Majesties," Alden said.

"Name it."

"Your promise was that he who solved the riddle could claim the hand of one of your daughters."

Reginald's eyebrows went up. "I thought you had said that your heart was given to another."

Alden nodded. "My heart has indeed been given to a woman of great beauty and character. I did not know when I pledged my heart to her that she was the Princess Electra." Alden extended his hand to Electra.

Electra stood and walked to Alden.

"Is this true, daughter?" Reginald said.

"It is," Electra said as she joined Alden. "We met in the city, where I have worked during the day at the coin exchange. No one knew my heritage. Alden did not know who I was or my true name until the ball."

Alden took out the chain and opened the locket to show Reginald and Beatrice. "She gave me this."

As they examined it, Electra said, "I did."

Beatrice turned to Electra. "Is your heart given to this man?"

Electra took Alden's hand and smiled. "It is."

Alden bowed to the royal couple. "I therefore ask for the great honor of your daughter's hand in marriage."

Reginald stood, leaned over the table, took Alden's and Electra's hands, and joined them. "I give my daughter Electra's hand in marriage to you, Alden. I expect you to conduct yourself with the same honor you have already shown."

"Gladly, Your Majesty."

Beatrice took a gold ring from her finger and handed it to Alden. "I wanted my eldest daughter to have this when it came time for her to marry."

Alden took the ring and bowed again. "Thank you, Your Majesty." He turned to Electra. "Will you marry me, Your Royal Highness?"

"I will. And will you marry me, Alden?"

"I will." Alden put the ring on Electra's finger. They joined hands and touched their foreheads together.

"Your Majesty," a voice said. "I have solved the riddle of the princesses."

Not a moment too soon, Alden thought. If he had arrived a minute later, Nevarth would have had the advantage.

Alden let Electra go and stood squarely between her and Nevarth. He was as the men at the inn described him: richly dressed, tall. Short hair, evenly golden. His chiseled face could have been carved out of stone. As with the other Enchanters, no flaws on his skin.

"You are too late," Alden told him. "The oath has been fulfilled."

The seated princesses all pushed back their chairs and stood.

Reginald faced Nevarth. "And who are you?"

Nevarth turned from Alden to Reginald. "I am the rightful ruler of this realm."

Reginald laughed.

Alden had been keeping his eyes on Nevarth, but when he surveyed the room now, he found that the princesses had vanished. The musicians and the royal couple remained with him and Nevarth.

"You doubt my power?" Nevarth said.

Alden strode to within a pace of Nevarth, facing him and putting himself between Nevarth and the royal couple. "There is more than one kind of power," he said with a confidence he did not feel. What he did feel was a mixture of great fear and great anger. The anger won out.

Nevarth looked Alden up and down. "Power? You? You are a pustulant worm that I would not soil my shoe to step on."

Alden lifted his chin and looked him straight in the eye. "I see that you have traveled far and learned words. I, too, have traveled far and learned words, you putrid degenerate miscreant."

"Your wit is as decayed as the rags you wear."

"The clothes I wear are from a day of honest labor in support of a widowed man and a provider of food for those who come inside after a day of hard work. I daresay yours are the unearned spoils of labors of others."

Alden felt a nudge. Out of the corner of his eye, he saw that the princesses had returned, wearing their dancing clothes and, for the first time, tiaras. Electra stood beside him, unfastening his outer shirt. He cooperated in the shirt's removal to keep his concentration on Nevarth.

"Your kind is born to be despoiled," Nevarth sneered. "You put up statues to conquerors."

"My kind makes statues of a man who was born in poverty and compassionate to all. My kind makes statues of a man who stepped down from his princely heritage and preached kindness and simplicity. Some of my kind make no statues at all to discourage men from worshiping other men as gods."

As he spoke, Electra removed his pants, leaving him in his underdrawers. Almost as quickly, she dressed him in the clothes the Enchanters had given him.

"I have thousands who obey my every word," Nevarth said, also seeming to ignore the princesses re-clothing and re-shoeing Alden as they argued.

Alden leaned left, looking around Nevarth, and then right, doing the same. Facing Nevarth again, he said, "Your followers must be unseen, or do you command an army of fleas?"

"The armies I commanded have made others quake in fear."

"I have free souls behind me who care for and defend their fellows of their own free will."

"I inflame ambitions."

"I move hearts."

"I have magic."

"So do we." Now completely transformed, Alden took Electra's hand and began to dance. The other princesses joined in. As they moved, Alden noted that Juno, wearing her own dress of enchanter cloth, had joined them.

The musicians, as the musicians at the city square earlier, seemed to know the tune and started playing.

Nevarth surveyed the moves and attempted to cut in. Alden spotted the attempt. Without missing a step, he drifted toward Nevarth and pulled him away. Nevarth wove his way into the assembly but found the others dancing away from him and out of his reach. He rushed Olympia, making a grab for her, but Reginald powered his way toward Nevarth and intercepted him. For a few moments, Nevarth and Reginald circled each other on the floor, in time to the music. Nevarth pushed Reginald away only to have Beatrice grasp both of Nevarth's hands and pull him away from the dance line.

All this time, Alden turned his head as he danced to keep Nevarth in view. Nevarth's face appeared to twist and turn purple. At first, Alden thought this was a trick of the light, but then Nevarth's skin began to peel off, first in flakes, and then in chunks. Nevarth did not bleed, but the exposed parts also turned a deep purple.

Nevarth seemed oblivious to this change, maintaining his efforts to join the dancers. Beatrice and Reginald acted equally determined to keep him away, passing him from one to the other, trying to engage him in a dance of their own.

Then, Nevarth shrank. Or, at least, seemed to. Beatrice and Reginald backed away from Nevarth and stared at the area of the floor where he had stood. The music faded away as the musicians stopped and stared. Alden felt a strong urge to halt and did. The princesses and Juno ceased dancing at the same instant.

Alden walked to where Nevarth had been. All that remained of him was a set of clothes strewn with purple ash.

"We're free!" Rhea shouted triumphantly.

Alden turned to Rhea, then Electra, who put a hand over her heart. She nodded. "Yes, I feel it, too."

"It's as if I have shed a great weight I didn't know I was carrying," Thalia said.

Reginald looked from the ash to the others. "What do we do with...this?" He waved a hand over the remains.

"Leave it for now," Electra said. "We'll ask the Enchanters what to do when we see them next." She walked away from the remains; the others followed.

When they reached a discreet distance of what was left of Nevarth, Beatrice said, "You have seen the Enchanters?"

"Of course," Rhea said. "Every night."

"You know them," Beatrice said.

"We do," Olympia said. "They know us."

"For my part," Lark said, "I married an Enchanter."

"You're married?" Reginald said, astonished.

"And you didn't invite us?" Beatrice asked, sounding disappointed.

"We couldn't talk about it until now," Rhea said.

"You couldn't wait?" Beatrice asked.

"I was with child," Lark said.

"I knew it," Beatrice said softly.

"You have a granddaughter," Lark said. "We named her Astra."

"You withheld our granddaughter from us?" Reginald said. "Knowing how we longed for a grandchild?"

"Father," Rhea said, "we could not talk about it."

Alden, standing aside listening to the conversation, put a hand over his mouth to hide a grin. Beatrice and Reginald had interrogated Lark in much the same way that Sherian and Lunaria had questioned Elenath.

Reginald turned from Rhea to Lark. "Now that you can talk about it, how about introducing us? And where's the father?"

"Here," Elenath said.

Chapter 11

They turned to see Elenath among a group of Enchanters standing at the doorway. He held the baby in his arms.

"I regret the delay," Zara said. "Nevarth put a barrier between us to hide from us that he had slipped in. We did not know until the barrier vanished. We came as soon as we could."

Electra extended her hand toward the remains. "That's what's left of him."

The Enchanters walked to the pile of ash and clothes, formed a circle around it, knelt, and bowed their heads. The others in the room remained where they were in respectful silence.

Zara stood first. She turned to the others. "We mourn the bright being he could have become, the waste of his talents, the harm he did to those outside this realm."

"He seemed to crumble before our eyes," Alden said.

"That was due to his gathering the last of his magic to oppose you," Wessalor said. "The effort consumed him."

Reginald approached Wessalor. "Is there a dignified way we can deal with the remains?"

"I'm a jeweler," Ilona said. "I have a suitable size box in my room." She stepped away and disappeared.

Beatrice raised both arms. "How do you do that?" she asked, exasperated.

"Being confined to the castle," Thalia said, "gave us a lot of time to learn how the enchantment worked."

"There was a lot of experimentation," Electra said. "We didn't learn it all at once. It took us years."

"...and working together," Rhea added.

Lunaria stepped next to Beatrice. "We have wondered for a long time whether our friends outside our realm could use magic.

The castle has remained enchanted, and the residents here have had varying successes in navigating the enchantment through the centuries. When your daughters proved their ability to use the magic here at will, we knew that our neighbors, though not able to originate magic, could manipulate magic already generated."

Elenath stepped closer. "Those in close touch with magic, here, or in the enchanted forest, could use it most easily."

Ilona reappeared with a large jeweled box. To Alden, it resembled a treasure chest. She handed it to Wessalor, who whisked Nevarth's remains into it and disappeared.

Meanwhile, Beatrice and Reginald moved closer to Elenath… and the baby.

Lark stepped up to them. "Your grandchild, Astra," she said to her parents.

Elenath smiled and handed the baby to Beatrice, who beamed, as did Reginald, looking over her shoulder.

Lark faced her parents and placed a hand on Elenath's shoulder. "This is my husband, Elenath."

Elenath executed an elegant bow. "Your Majesties."

Lark indicated two of the Enchanters. "And these are Elenath's parents, Sherian and Lunaria."

Both sets of grandparents exchanged respectful nods. Alden, looking on, guessed that Elenath's intention was to show regard to his in-laws, while Reginald and Beatrice and the Enchanters recognized each other as fellow grandparents.

Reginald faced Sherian. "I suppose you knew about this marriage and birth long ago."

"No," Sherian said. "We did not know about this until very recently. We would have wished to have been told sooner."

"As would we." Reginald turned to Elenath. "What do you have to say for yourself, young man?"

"Father," Lark said, "Elenath is older than you are."

"He's not older than we are," Lunaria said.

Electra had been holding hands with Alden. Without releasing her grip, she stepped toward the assembly. "Elenath has worked the hardest to bring us to a point where we could all speak freely. He deserves praise for that."

"He has done the honorable thing by marrying Lark and seeing to her and their child's welfare," Alden added.

"I understand the need to question me," Elenath said.

Lark faced both sets of parents. "Elenath and I would have married even if I hadn't been with child."

"In that case, I withdraw my challenge." Reginald turned to Elenath. "Welcome to the family, son."

Elenath smiled. "Thank you."

Reginald turned to Alden and Electra, who still held hands. "I hope that you won't run off and marry without us being there."

"The thought never entered my mind," Electra said.

"What about you, Alden?" Reginald asked.

"In this matter, I will be guided by my bride."

Reginald turned to Rhea and Juno, who stood together. "Have you added a sister, Rhea?"

Rhea smiled and took Juno's hand. "Not a sister, Father."

Reginald walked over to them. "Are you handfasted?"

Rhea and Juno turned to each other. Rhea turned back to Reginald. "No."

"Would you like to be?" Reginald asked.

Juno beamed and turned to Rhea.

"Yes," Rhea said.

Reginald walked over and took Juno's hand. "I may not have had eyes to see, but I recognize you as the seamstress who has provided the court with many a handsome outfit, and though you may have been masked in my eyes, I recognized your bearing when you danced with Rhea just now. It is the same bearing of the woman Rhea has danced with at many a ball. I saw how you looked at each other and knew that Rhea had given her heart to you, and you to her." With his other hand, he took Rhea's and placed it over Juno's. "I bestow to you Rhea's hand. May your union be blessed."

Both women let out an exclamation of delight and kissed.

"I expect that the two of you won't run off," Reginald added in a low voice.

Juno laughed delightedly. "No, but I've always imagined a small, quiet gathering...pledging my troth with my love in a forest, among the falling leaves."

"I've never wanted a lot of pageantry, either." Rhea turned from Juno to the Enchanters. "I know of a place that has gold and silver leaves, which fall all seasons of the year."

"Once Juno becomes accustomed to our magic, we would be happy to make arrangements for you," Zara offered.

Alden turned to Electra. "My love, nothing would give me more pleasure than to remain in your company. But the men at Quentin's are expecting my return. Besides, I'm famished."

"We have food," Alinora said. The triplets looked identical, but each wore an embroidered ribbon bearing her name.

Beatrice, still holding Astra, approached. "I was given to believe that brandy was your occupation."

Arabella snorted. "You know how people talk. No, we're dairy maids."

"We make cheese," Alesia said.

"Good cheese," Alinora agreed.

"We deliver it to the kitchen daily," Arabella said.

"In disguise," Alesia added.

"With deference to your cheese, sisters," Electra said, "Alden has other obligations to fulfill. There are uncounted days ahead when he can sample your wares."

Alden kissed Electra's hand and bowed to the assembly. He was about to walk out when Electra said, "Don't you think you ought to change first?"

He stopped and looked down, realizing he was wearing the clothes made of enchanter cloth.

Electra handed him his everyday clothes and pointed to a place sectioned off at a corner of the room. "You can change there. Leave your new clothes on a seat. I'll take them."

He bowed again to the assembly and went to change. When he emerged, Electra escorted him to the door. They exchanged a brief kiss there before he stepped into the hallway.

At the entrance, he encountered Silas, who asked, "Did you lose your way? We somehow got separated. I looked for you but couldn't find you."

"No, I was able to speak to Their Majesties, thank you. And now I'm returning to the city."

"How were you received?" Silas asked.

"Very well, thank you."

When Alden opened the door to Quentin and Matilda's, he saw a crowd there, in addition to the regulars.

Deval approached him. "That man, that man was here. We tried to talk to him...."

"...we all tried," Quentin said.

"...but when he talked, all of a sudden, it was as if we forgot what we were going to say. Then he left, and by the time we recovered our wits, he was long out the door and it was too late to stop him."

Alden put a hand on Deval's shoulder. "Don't worry. All is well. That was an Enchanter. You and everyone else here fell under his spell."

"An Enchanter?" Bennu said.

"Nevarth," Alden said.

"Nevarth? I thought he was only a legend." Gerasim looked around the room as if to confirm the others might think so, too.

"The Enchanters have to be real," Bennu said, "because we see evidence of them all the time. But the characters the storytellers talk about...I thought they were made up."

Alden smiled and shook his head slightly. "No, they are real, all of them, and I have met them."

"Nevarth?" Quentin said. "Isn't he a danger to us all?"

Alden nodded. "But not anymore. He died."

"Don't tell me you killed him," Quentin said.

"I did not," Alden said. "His own magic consumed him."

Gerasim pulled an empty chair from a table. "You must sit and tell us all about it."

"I will, another time. First, I must eat. I'm famished." He lowered himself into the chair.

"Sit, then." Quentin called to the back. "Matilda! Dinner for our friend Alden."

Within a minute, a server came with a plate of food and utensils and set them in front of Alden. While he sat and ate, the regulars watched over him. Quentin busied himself with other diners, who spoke quietly among themselves as they stole glances at Alden from time to time.

When Alden finished his meal, and took a last sip of cider, Bennu spoke before Alden set the mug down again.

"Come, Alden, tell us."

Alden smiled. "Like the legendary storyteller of old, I need to tell the story in parts. I have to stop at the residence and check on Jacob soon."

"Then tell us something. Anything," Gerasim said.

"Philippa's father bestowed her hand in marriage. We are officially betrothed."

The room broke out in applause and cries of "Congratulations!" Several people slapped him on the back or patted his shoulder.

"And there's the bride," Gerasim called, extending his arm.

Alden turned to the door and saw Philippa standing there, beaming, dressed in a modest court gown. He rose from the chair, walked to her, and took her hand.

Deval's brow furrowed. "No, that's the Princess Electra."

"I am Philippa and I am the Princess Electra," she said. "The enchantment at the palace kept those who saw me from realizing that I am both. That spell is now broken."

The door opened behind them. Alden turned to see Olympia walk in. She also wore a court gown.

"Princess Olympia," Deval said.

"No, that's Signe," Quentin said.

"Again, both," Alden said.

"I and all of my sisters took occupations in the city or countryside," Electra said. "After all, our parents will not reign forever. We needed to pursue our own passions."

"You've seen Queen Beatrice," Alden said to Deval.

"Yes."

Alden turned from Deval to Electra. "Do you not see the resemblance?"

Deval turned to Electra.

She moved closer to him and held out a hand. "You're familiar with the queen's ring? She gave it to Alden to put on my hand to seal our betrothal."

Deval bowed. "Your Highness."

Matilda and the rest of the kitchen folk had stepped out into the main room. "Are you still going to be at the coin exchange?" Matilda asked.

"When it opens tomorrow morning," Philippa affirmed.

Matilda smiled and nodded.

"And I will be at Jacob's carpentry shop." He turned to Electra. "I am going to check on Jacob now."

"I'll go with you," Electra said.

"I'll stay here," Olympia said. "I'm sure there will be a lot of questions."

Alden nodded. "They'll spread the word. You know how people talk."

Olympia chuckled.

Alden and Electra found Sister Angelica standing at the entrance to the residence when they arrived.

"The prayer meeting ended a short time ago," she said. "I was just making my farewells to the last of the worshippers. All of a sudden, while we were praying, everyone's spirits rose. At once. It was a miracle."

Alden and Electra exchanged a smile. "I won't argue with that," he said.

"Your prayers are greatly appreciated," Electra said. "The danger is over."

Sister Angelica nodded. "We all could feel it. We don't know exactly how, but a great peace moved among us."

"I don't doubt it," Alden said.

"You'll surely hear all about it in the coming days," Electra said. "Though it's too long a story to tell right now."

Sister Angelica smiled. "I can wait."

"I presume Jacob is still playing cards?" Alden said.

"Never stopped." Sister Angelica gestured inside. "Please, come in."

Alden and Electra started toward the common room. While passing through the hallways, they heard murmurs from others they saw along the way, presumably when they recognized a princess among them.

The door to the common room was open. Alden and Electra walked right in and stood behind Jacob. The card players, intent on their game, paid them little notice.

Alden waited until they had finished a hand to speak. "How is it going?"

"Won some, lost some." Jacob sounded satisfied.

"How's the mood?" Alden prompted.

One of the players raised a beer mug. Alden noticed each player had a mug by his side.

"Couldn't be better," said the player.

Without looking back, Jacob said, "Just a cloud passing by. I don't know what I was worried about before."

"I'm going home from here," Alden said. "Did you want to stay overnight?"

"No, I'll go with you." Jacob pushed his chair back and turned in Alden's direction briefly. "Oh, hello, Philippa." He turned back to the other players. "Thanks, folks. I had a great time."

One of the players said, "Us, too. Come back anytime, Jacob."

Another of the players leaned over and whispered loudly. "That's the Princess Electra, Jacob."

Jacob stood and turned around. "No, that's Philippa."

A third player gestured in her direction. "I think you're both right."

"They are," Electra said with a smile.

Jacob faced Electra. "You're a princess?"

"Yes, Jacob, I am."

"Well, you aren't as spoiled as I always thought you were. Good for you for taking a job."

The player that whispered tugged Jacob's shirt. "Probably shouldn't speak to a princess that way."

Electra turned to the player. "Oh, that's all right. Jacob and I are old friends. Thank you for keeping him company."

The other players all rose from their chairs, bowed, and sat again.

Jacob retrieved his pack and walked out with Alden and Philippa. Once they were on the street, he looked at Philippa's hand. "You're betrothed?"

"Yes, Jacob, we are," Philippa said, "and there are plenty of rooms in the castle, and plenty of people to talk to. You won't be alone. You can move in when we get married."

"What about the shop?" Jacob said.

"You and I can still go to the shop every day," Alden said.

"And we can arrange for a carriage to bring you there," Electra said.

"Can we still go fishing?" Jacob said to Alden.

"Yes, we can," Alden said. "Though you understand that once I'm married, I'll be eating dinner with my wife."

"You can eat with us, too, occasionally," Electra said, "but you can also have dinner with Quentin and Matilda before going back to the castle. You'll see Deval and Bennu there from time to time, and I'm sure you'll get along with the castle carpenters."

"Will the castle carpenters welcome another?"

"Of course," Electra said, "and they have a well-equipped shop to work in. You can work there, too, if you wish, in addition to keeping up your own shop."

Jacob looked thoughtful.

When they reached Jacob's home, Alden said, "I'm walking Electra back to the castle. I'll be back shortly."

"You aren't going to be out all night?" Jacob asked.

"Not tonight. I'll return as soon as Electra is back at the castle."

Jacob nodded.

Word did spread fast. Soon everyone knew the story of the princesses and Nevarth. The princesses continued to go to their usual jobs. Electra reported being treated with a little more deference, but that was all. Alden, as Electra's betrothed, noticed more knowing smiles among the customers who came to the shop.

The princesses and Alden continued going to the Enchanters' castle to dance, but only once a week, and they brought Reginald, Beatrice, and Juno, who gradually became used to the magic. The princesses no longer wore out their shoes every night. Alden checked with Jin and Li, who said they still had plenty of orders for shoes, and added that to be truthful, they were relieved at the lighter work load.

Once Juno and Reginald and Beatrice became used to the magic, Alden attended a lovely ceremony for Rhea and Juno under the enchanted trees. Zara led them through uniting vows as gold and silver leaves floated down among the assembly. The couple wore elegant embroidered gowns and each wore an elaborate flower crown.

Once they had kissed, Beatrice approached Juno with a small, gem-encrusted box that Alden suspected had been made by Ilona.

"Since you are family now," Beatrice said, "This is for you."

Juno took the box, opened it, and smiled. She reached in and brought out a tiara.

"Thank you," Juno said.

"It's traditional to give a title when royal offspring marry," Reginald said. "You are now our daughter...and our princess."

Juno smiled. "I don't know when I'd wear this, though."

"You wear it to our wedding," Electra said, with a knowing look to Alden.

Alden and Electra planned a traditional wedding. Alden felt his princely outfit, sewn from enchanted cloth, was matchless, and Electra agreed. Juno and Rhea worked on Electra's wedding outfit, which Alden did not see constructed, but was told had wide skirts and a long veil. Electra seemed to be delighted with the progress.

The wedding was to take place in the main hall at the castle. Alden and Electra asked Reverend Whitcomb to perform the ceremony. Juno and Rhea sewed and embroidered a special robe for him to wear. Electra was to have the princesses as her attendants. Alden asked Jacob to be his best man and selected the regulars at the inn plus Elenath to be his attendants. Quentin and Matilda declined the offer to be attendants but accepted the invitation to be witnesses at the wedding. Jin and Li also received invitations.

Alden had attended weddings of his brothers and sisters, and was no stranger to the ceremony. Reverend Whitcomb advised a rehearsal nonetheless, which went well. On the day of the wedding, Alden led his attendants up the steps and onto the dais. He looked out over the substantial crowd, which included several Enchanters. They seemed to be in a joyous mood.

Jacob leaned toward him. "Nervous?"

"Not greatly, no."

Elenath smiled. "The castle's enchantment is calming."

"For which I am grateful," Alden said.

The musicians struck up a tune. The princesses, including Juno, slowly strode into the room and up the stairs to stand opposite Alden and his attendants. They all wore tiaras and dazzling clothes fashioned of enchanter cloth.

Electra entered the room on Reginald's arm. Her wedding dress also seemed to be sewn from enchanter cloth. She wore a tiara under the veil, and he could see her smiling as she approached.

There was no sermon, just the ceremony. Alden and Electra had chosen vows similar to what Alden had heard was the Methodist tradition, where the bride did not pledge to obey, though Electra said when Alden remarked on it that brides in this realm seldom made that pledge.

At the end of the ceremony, Whitcomb invited them to kiss. After they did, they signed the wedding certificate on a nearby lectern. Reginald and Beatrice applied the royal seal. Reginald then surprised Alden by taking a gold coronet from a pillow that had been left on a chair next to the lectern. He faced the crowd.

"It is traditional for the spouse of a monarch to be given a title. In this case, the man that my daughter has married has worked hard for the good of this realm and its people. He has more than earned the title of Prince of the Realm." He placed the crown on Alden's head.

Alden bowed. "I'm honored, Your Majesties."

The crowd cheered.

Electra beamed.

As had been rehearsed, Alden took Electra's hand and walked down the stairs. No one else moved while Alden escorted Electra to the door and through the hallways to the castle entrance, where an open coach awaited them. Since there were far more people interested in the wedding than could be seated in the main hall, the coach was to make a circuit around the city and return to the castle.

People had lined up on both side of the streets, waving and cheering. Some threw flowers. Alden and Electra waved back and occasionally kissed, to the delight of the crowd.

When they returned to the castle, the hall had been cleared of most of the people. Only family and a few invited guests had remained for a wedding banquet and dance.

As they moved through the steps of the music, Electra leaned toward Alden. "You seem to be popular."

"Oh, I'm sure it's you they were cheering, and rightfully so."

"You're too modest, husband. I've been asked at the coin exchange whether you or I or both of us will try to lift the crown when my parents retire."

"Jacob told me he's heard the same. I'm honored by the confidence in me, though I have to admit that I had never considered it as an occupation."

"There's a saying in this realm that those who seek power the least are the ones who rule the best."

Alden nodded. "A wise saying, and one that generally matches my experience in the world."

"We'll have time enough to contemplate the idea, I think."

"Agreed. I had planned on going back to work at Jacob's shop during the day once our expected honeymoon is over."

Electra chuckled. "And I planned to stay at the coin shop for a good long time. The brothers still can't balance a ledger."

"Besides that, there are the weekly dances with the Enchanters, and I presume you'll want to continue the Sunday dances...."

"...of course. Life goes on as it always has."

"I think everyone would notice if it didn't. You know how people talk."

Acknowledgments

I wish to extend my sincere thanks to the members of my critique group, Elizabeth Rowan Keith, Eleanor Dorn, Ellen Kuhfeld, Monica Ferris, Ted Schoep, P.C. Hodgell, and the late Ann Peters for their invaluable advice and encouragement as I wrote this novel.

I also wish to thank Gayle S. Stever for her generous support.

About the Author

Joan Marie Verba is an autistic author, publisher, and web developer with a bachelor's degree in physics. She was an associate instructor of astronomy for one year. She has worked as a computer programmer, web developer, editor, publisher, and social media manager. An experienced writer, she is the author of fiction and nonfiction books plus numerous short stories and articles. Her novels have received the Mom's Choice Award® and the Scribe Award. She is a member of the Science Fiction and Fantasy Writers Association and the International Association of Media Tie-in Writers.

Joan has a newsletter which comes out every two weeks. Sign up at her website: joanmarieverba.com

Joan's Twitter page: @joanmarieverba

Made in the USA
Columbia, SC
05 September 2022

66341716R00080